Nosy

White

Woman

A John Metcalf Book

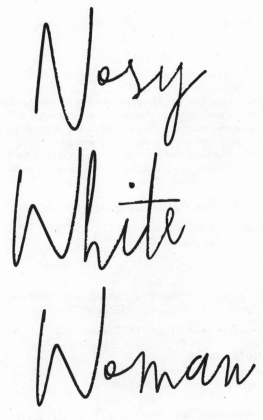

Nosy White Woman

Stories

Martha Wilson

Biblioasis
Windsor, Ontario

Library and Archives Canada Cataloguing in Publication

Wilson, Martha, 1964–, author
Nosy white woman / Martha Wilson.

Short stories

Issued in print and electronic formats.
Canadiana (print) 20189044659 | Canadiana (ebook) 20189044667
ISBN 9781771962896 (softcover) | ISBN 9781771962902 (ebook)

LCC PS3623.I4778 G65 2019 | DDC 813/.6—dc23

Edited by John Metcalf
Copy-edited by Allana Amlin
Cover and text designed by Gordon Robertson

Canada Council for the Arts · Conseil des Arts du Canada

ONTARIO CREATES | ONTARIO CRÉATIF

Canada

ONTARIO ARTS COUNCIL
CONSEIL DES ARTS DE L'ONTARIO
an Ontario government agency
un organisme du gouvernement de l'Ontario

Published with the generous assistance of the Canada Council for the Arts, which last year invested $153 million to bring the arts to Canadians throughout the country, and the financial support of the Government of Canada. Biblioasis also acknowledges the support of the Ontario Arts Council (OAC), an agency of the Government of Ontario, which last year funded 1,709 individual artists and 1,078 organizations in 204 communities across Ontario, for a total of $52.1 million, and the contribution of the Government of Ontario through the Ontario Book Publishing Tax Credit and Ontario Creates.

PRINTED AND BOUND IN CANADA

Dedicated to the therapists, DeWitt Crosby and John Keller, who taught me to keep asking, "What does this remind me of?"

————

And to the oncology team—Lucy Helyer, Tallal Younis, Lisa Cicchelli, and Maureen Nolan—who saved my life. I'm grateful every day.

As we drove through hundreds of trees heavy with hanging branches of green leaves, I began to wonder what it was like to live around there.

— Julie Hecht, *Do the Windows Open?*

Oh, Earth, you are a lucky planet.

— Nicholson Baker, *Substitute*

Contents

The Voice of Furniture

When I was fifteen my father was struck by the notion that it must be mystifyingly difficult, or impossible, to create a Chinese dictionary.

I heard him say it twice, which means he ran through that routine probably a dozen times. "I've been wondering recently. In Chinese they write with characters. Every word's a kind of picture. So how would you make a dictionary?" Extravagantly pleased with himself, beaming around whatever group with smug charm. That big bald head and expansive geniality. And a person or two chiming in to muse—True; how would you, indeed. His pleasure seemed to derive equally from having had the insight and from the exotic flavour of his question: the Silk Road; bicycles. Coolie hats.

"You couldn't make a dictionary without an alphabet," he would elaborate. "Right? Some form of alphabet. So how would you do it? You couldn't."

Clever, and proud of it; that was how my whole family was, but especially my father. Always the smartest adult in the room, he took it for granted from my babyhood on that I, inheritor of his genes, was therefore the smartest child in the room; other parents thought their own children were, but he and I knew better.

The Chinese-dictionary conundrum is one I remember because of his erroneous initial premise, that you need an alphabet in order to generate a dictionary, and because he jumped so effortlessly to the conclusion that if he didn't know how and couldn't easily imagine a way, it couldn't be done.

This was around 1980, but we did have methods of transmitting knowledge. Canada wasn't wilderness. We had encyclopedias. We had libraries filled with books, some of which were about other countries. It would have been more difficult back then, but not impossible, to gain familiarity with the concept of stroke order—that strokes are supposed to be written in a certain progression, which means there's a prescribed structure within a character-based writing system. It's not like dropping a fistful of toothpicks on the table. That fact was known in the world in 1980, even by some in the West. There are several methods for organizing such dictionaries, and they go back a couple of thousand years.

My father's question was really, I think, a lack of curiosity masquerading as a search for knowledge—like any other incidence of saying, "Huh, how'd you do that," while not caring what the response might be. He wasn't prompting his acquaintances to ponder the written communication of Japan and China and Korea, he was giving an audience a good stumper.

His whole family seemed to relish any sort of little rhetorical performance. One of his brothers, my American uncle, liked a game gleaned from the *Reader's Digest* that involved asking someone he was paying (usually young, usually a girl he could fluster), "Do you take Hawaiian money?" I've met a couple of other people my age whose older relatives, men of a jokey, pedantic mindset, used to go around confronting people with that question. (It was when everyone subscribed to *Reader's Digest*; the U.S. version, especially, hid a fierce right-wing agenda behind the innocent pleasantries of Laughter, the Best Medicine.) Bands of middle-aged white men were, presumably, all over the place back then, demanding whether various establishments took Hawaiian money. Then came the surprised or dismayed "I . . . don't know, sir. I'll have to ask the manager." Followed by the climax: "There's no such thing as Hawaiian money! Hawaii's a state, so their money is the same as the rest of the country's!"

Pellets of knowledge, given out freely. The man's querulous enjoyment of the other person's discomfort. These were people skilled at fitting a glancing reprimand or a quick lecture in nearly anywhere, people who enjoyed scolding strangers. How quick you'd need to be, to have a hope of shooting back, "Hawaiian money doesn't exist!"

Either quick, or to have heard that one before.

Though even if you hadn't, you'd know something was up. Such men came in various guises, but they shared a testy sense of ownership you could see coming, if you were alert. Dread was what you felt, once you realized they were ready to launch into whatever their current trick was. We never seemed able to ask the simple question, "Why are you entitled to try to make a fool of me?"

Last Thursday evening I ended up at McDonald's for a Garden Task Force meeting. I'm on this town beautification committee (tapped because I manage the garden centre at the hardware store), and only the committee chair and I arrived at the Community Room upstairs at the grocery store for our bulb planning session. It seemed chilly there, the two of us at that exaggeratedly white table in a white-tiled room, so we decided to walk across the parking lot and get something. I'd already eaten but I do like those little pies they have, and I'm a person who could drink coffee at midnight and not have trouble sleeping.

Grant ordered McMuffins and fries, and told me he hadn't had a chance to rustle up dinner yet. (I took this to mean he also lived by himself. No doubt partly because he talked like someone on *Bonanza*.) The counter girl put his ham treat on the tray and told him she'd bring the sausage one to our table.

"You should have been serving all-day breakfast all along," Grant said. "This is what people really want."

She didn't bother to answer this, so I did. "Breakfast for dinner," I said. "My brothers and I always liked that when we were kids."

"Don't you find?" he asked her. "That the all-day breakfast is pretty popular?"

"Yeah, people like it," she said. "I'll bring your Sausage McMuffin out to you."

Grant and I got a table by the glassed-in fireplace that sported a low row of blue flames, uniform as the teeth of a comb. Without actually offering heat, it looked as if it were about to. I couldn't understand what I was seeing. Was it a real fireplace, or not? The flames were right there, flickering, not LEDs like all the battery-operated candles now, but the glass was cold. I felt foolish for trying to huddle up to an unmistakably not-warm fixture. We spread our things about, crinkling paper and doctoring up our food. Grant peppered his egg slab and put the top back on.

These places used to be busy at night, but that era is over. There was a young couple across the room, clearly fighting in undertones, and closer to this side were two grandparents with children dipping fries in ketchup and saying, "Look, Nan! A birthday candle!" I remembered when McDonald's used to report their rising burger count on their outdoor signs, before they gave up, fatigued by their success, and just went with, "Billions and billions served," and I thought how many hundreds of thousands of preschoolers had tipped their fries with ketchup and called them candles. And the "Look, Nan!"—I remembered that, as well: how I used to address only my grandmother even though I meant Pop, too. My grandfather was the silent presence, communicating through her.

Carrie from the counter approached with Grant's other sandwich. His maguffin, as I called them when I was little.

"Thank you, young lady," he said. "Are you the manager for this shift?"

"Uh, no, I'm not," she said.

"Well, I would like to have you give the manager a message for me."

"All right," she said doubtfully.

"I would like you to tell him, or her, that McDonald's should have been serving breakfast in the evening all along. I am much more likely to come here now."

"Okay," she said.

The thought of Grant, unable to face rustling up his own dinner and feeling now more likely to drive to McDonald's for some breakfast sandwiches, made me want to weep.

And yet. I took little nibbles from the corners of my rectangular pie. I couldn't relate to any belief that a complaint or instruction will filter up and be heard, that there are only a couple of layers between you and the top of an organization and that your input is sought and will be valued. While the rest of us know: Nobody cares what you think.

I have to be careful about sadness. There's a tendency now to let things get to me. It's a lesson I've learned a bunch of times before, but I can get drawn in, because the small tragedies are, these days, kind of pre-verified. There are twin kinds of sadness on the outskirts of this mood, and both are dangerous.

The first is a tender leakage I feel in the presence of poignant significance: if I see an insect attending to its busy schedule, say, with all of its necessary, matter-of-fact courage intact; or something like a very young tree with three fragile leaves, still translucent; or a little handiwork project that received too much care and attention. Or occasionally when you're out shopping you notice someone—an *adult*; this kills me—breaking in the thing they've just bought. Adjusting a hatband, say, so they can wear their new cap around the mall. Smoothing the backs of a new pair of gloves with a kind of soft wonder. I can't stand to see people so exposed; almost awed by their purchases, and optimistic that some change will now begin to unfold. Hoping they'll look as cool in their sunglasses as they imagined.

The other dangerous sadness for me is to get walloped by despair when faced with the unfortunate outcome of a decision someone made. This gloom first descended on me in a Big Boy restaurant decades ago, dumb-struck by a terrible light fixture and thinking through the steps involved: someone designed that thing, someone approved it, someone manufactured it, someone ordered it, and someone installed it. Drained of all hope, I wanted to crawl under the banquette and lapse into a coma.

Both sadnesses are trouble, I've come to realize. Even though they're legitimate, they're also warning bells that signal depression, and they mean I'm at risk of veering off the path. And ever since the U.S. abandoned all democratic norms and guardrails to let that fat fool take office, I've had to keep a close eye on my warning signals.

So I was wary of the sympathetic instincts I felt around Grant's inability or unwillingness to scratch up some dinner for himself. Picturing him blank and tragic in a kitchen with a yellow ceiling fixture and a black window over the sink, I didn't want to toughen my heart; but I told myself it was necessary. Ignore the thought of his sad cupboards. My mind tends to fill in all this pitiable aching, but Grant's a grown man. He can make a goddamn sandwich.

If I perhaps inspired sympathetic compassion in Grant, if he pictured me alone in my kitchen making a BLT with limp lettuce, he wasn't showing it. He evinced no curiosity about me whatsoever: not who my family was, how long I'd been at the hardware store, nothing. The polite question was not his strength—was, in fact, missing altogether from his skill set.

I live in one of those green duplexes beside the old high school. It's a six-minute walk to work, which is just enough to feel as if I've gotten a little exercise. Sure, someone might pity me. I do some cross-stitching, watch a little TV with my Roku device that gets everything. My Siamese, Patience, dozes on her side next to me, all four feet bunched together in a point, her closed eye just a dark checkmark.

The thing is, though, I've seen the coziness of these six apartments from the outside. My neighbours—Clint, and Bud and Julie, and everyone—we have lamps that shine from our windows and announce, We're here; we're on the phone to our mothers in Winnipeg or Fredericton; we're making beef stir-fry and mine-strone soup. We pop in and out. Patience wakes up to purr and goes back to sleep, purring; she's the shape of a salmon steak, or the Millennium Falcon, and I can rest my hand on her flank and she'll respond without waking. I garden around all three buildings and have taught everyone a little about weeding and watering; next summer we're doing daylilies.

So I told myself not to worry about what Grant thought of me. (Which was nothing, apparently.) We chose some bulbs from my catalogs and picked where they would go—fire hall; raised bed by the credit union; west edge of Victoria Park—and discussed how much of a discount I could wrangle for us. How many Rex, my boss, would throw in for free. Where we could store them after they were delivered, and whether older ones would be less likely to emerge.

A few years ago I had a chance to go with a team from the head office to Amsterdam during the tulip season. We took trips outside the city and visited their enormous nurseries, miles-long fields of blooms. I attended seminar sessions on field moisture levels and insect control, on fire fungus, blue mold, basal rot. It was my first trip to Europe, and I came back with two hopes: to do more travelling, and to move to Ottawa and get a job with the tulip festival people.

With a little distance it started seeming embarrassingly childish to me—I travelled one time, and then I wanted to travel more, plus find work in the very niche my travels had exposed me to! what a coincidence—and yet the wish was both honourable and persistent. I'm not looking hard, but I've set up alerts on job posting boards that will let me know when anything in that area comes up.

And now, sitting by an operating-but-heatless fireplace across from a guy who kept pointing a McMuffin at me to emphasize his words, I remembered that I was kind of the expert here. He was a former principal, a man used to setting the agenda and doling out little dollops of correction or retribution. (Bossy and high-handed, though not a bad person. Basically kind.) Yet I was the one here anticipating which problems might develop. I could talk about deer, squirrels, fungus, drainage.

"Let me tell you," he said.

A sudden spike in volume as a group of horse people swept in, on their way home from a practice or event. There was a din, and a lineup at the cash registers. They ranged from middle age down to children, and they kept reassembling themselves into different subgroups as they sorted through who was paying for whom. Some carried gear. Several women sported those equestrian socks in zany patterns that they wear with their jodhpurs, concealed by their boots until they switch to sneakers. I've often thought I'd like to wear something secret like that.

I asked Grant, "Is there a show at the Exhibition this week, do you know?"

He shook his head. "Not here. I think there may be one in Digby." He glanced at his watch.

Grant was finishing his coffee and watching them, idly, but with some hook to his gaze. They didn't seem unusual—just a group of rambunctious kids and worn-out adults. What was making his expression look like a poke? I glanced between the counter lineup and him. His gaze moved from person to person, his pale blue eyes seeming to tally, or calculate. Something in the lines of his face brought a memory of my own face back to me; I was seeing from the outside an expression I could remember having worn. He's figuring out whether they're all superior or inferior, I suddenly thought.

And I do remember that. I remember summing up each person I encountered and having to decide who was better than I was, who was not as good. It used to happen so quickly it was as if my amygdala were doing the sizing up for me, faster than my brain could think. With everyone.

What were the criteria I used? It's one of those things so remote in my memory I only know I used to do it, not how I went about it. Looks, obviously, and status. Confidence, or how confident the person seemed. Profession, intelligence, clothes—I had naïve but very set ideas about all these. Relationship status? Probably. It made for a complicated algebra that nonetheless had mostly predictable outcomes.

Since this spring, when I decided I was finished with dating married men, I've found my thoughts running farther back a lot. I spent eleven years on Ronald, and before that wasted two years on Jacob (also married).

Now I find I keep thinking about Jiro, the last unmarried man I had a serious relationship with.

Jiro was from a suburb of Tokyo and had gone to college in California, at UC Santa Cruz, where he spent four years surfing. Then he looked at graduate schools (he studied plankton) and ended up at Dalhousie, so he was able to spend his weekends at Lawrencetown Beach and do more surfing, albeit in a wetsuit. We met at my cousin's Canada Day barbecue.

He's long gone from my life, back in Tokyo or Yokohama or somewhere, and for years I hardly thought about him. But I remember we hadn't been seeing each other long when I told him about my way of assessing people, that I ranked everyone as superior or inferior to me, that I couldn't help it. Admitting it felt like a confession, something humiliating, even though I couldn't pinpoint what there was to be ashamed about.

What I remember now is how, when I talked about myself, he often just said, "Huh." But his eyes stayed fixed on my face, unsurprised, interested in hearing the next development. It was "huh" followed by curiosity, not "huh" followed by dismissal. We'd lie on the rug in his one-room condo in Halifax with our feet up on the sofa, playing with each other's hands. He told me about cormorant fishing, about Tokyo Disneyland, about skiing in Japan's alps, about learning to cook. He talked about his family, about his sister who once got so furious with their parents that she stayed away from home for three days; his parents had no idea where she was and were afraid she would become a prostitute. She came home and, after a time, settled down; now she was married and had a kindergartner and a baby. I told him about my after-school job at the deli during high school, about my tropical fish and how I was convinced my parents weren't taking the best care of them, about having had to take my driving test four times before I passed because parallel parking was killing me. I told him about church and the mall and middle school, about being in the hospital for pneumonia when I was seven, about how I used to read nothing but sci fi and now never read it at all.

He introduced me to an idea that I think originated with him, though perhaps it's a widely known concept in Japan. He called it the voice of furniture.

"I'll give you the example," he said, in his English that, while nearly perfect, was still accented and retained some idiosyncrasies. "Perhaps we're talking. Saying goodbye. But we talk for a few minutes; then we pause. Right? Then there's a small sound, not related to us—a truck, or a child playing somewhere. So one of us says, 'Well, I'd better go. I'll see you later.' Because that sound made us realize the world again, even if we don't know we heard it."

"Maybe sometimes," I said, "but not that often. Not every conversation."

"Every," he said. "Every. You watch."

I watched, and he was right. I saw that conversations surge and contract in response to this barely perceptible static, that people answer to unintended cues from the air. I became an avid tabulator of voice of furniture examples.

It was around that time, I believe, that I began to edge out of my automatic reckoning of other people as either superior or inferior to me. Even though that wasn't a habit I liked, I wasn't trying to snap myself out of doing it; yet somehow that worldview shifted, and some other screen or filter, invisible to me, moved into its place.

So I'd forgotten. I'd forgotten altogether my ongoing hum of distress, during those years I was compelled to compare myself to every living soul who crossed my path. I'd forgotten how exhausting it used to be. Was this what Grant was doing now? Was this how he lived, a man in his sixties, a white man in Canada who'd gotten nearly everything he ever wanted, the things he couldn't have small enough that the rest of us would consider them meaningless?

And how would he rank me? I figured I knew the answer to that one, though of course we're never certain what other people think. I'd been given a great gift, in not needing to care. I was like a knight in chess that had made a deft sideways move, a swoop that took me out of harm's way. I was still inclined to feel vaguely sorry for Grant, but I'd gotten it down to a pale, washed-out version of a distant pity, a pity that barely registered. And however he felt about me didn't affect me at all.

The voice of outside clatter came along to save me right then, as it so often does—one of those natural phenomena that we can rest in and rely on. The horse people swept through in noisy clumps, adults herding exhausted kids; they created a distraction and a segue. I looked down at my notes on bulbs and our sketched-out plans for the town's new beds.

"We've made a good start here," I said. "I think we can probably wrap up now."

Though there had been something in addition, a little spate of accord and teamwork, while we were choosing tulips. It was such a pleasant sorting and selecting. I'd felt it in spite of what I thought of his manners. The two of us had gone through the pages with a kind of delighted agreement, the way my sister and I used to turn slowly through the offerings of the toy catalog. The richness, and being able to pick. Angelique, Purple Majesty. Double Shirley. Guinevere. Wild Blue Heart.

The Pritzker Prize Livestream

"I could go alone. On the train." Teresa's daughter brought out this suggestion with an air of daring. All weekend Ruby, who was fourteen, had been begging Teresa to take her to an architecture conference in Toronto.

"I wouldn't mind your taking the train, but it's too far to go alone."

"Mom, I don't need a chaperone."

"Well, you can't go by yourself," Teresa said.

"Nothing would happen! Why don't you trust me? I thought you wanted me to learn to be independent. I would take the train to Union Station; catch the subway, which, by the way, I know how to do; and go straight to the conference, where I would sit in a big room and watch PowerPoints. So that is exactly like school, except actually interesting."

"Ruby, you cannot go alone. All you're proving right now is that your frontal lobe is undeveloped. Have you heard from your dad? Maybe he could take you, if it means so much."

Even more worked up, Ruby said, "He texted me back. He said, 'Well, we'll see,' so in other words, not a chance. And you know he'll have to work."

Teresa's resolve wavered a bit toward one side, like a flame. If Mark was going to oppose this, she felt almost obligated to act as a counterweight. Was he dismissing this idea of Ruby's as childish nonsense? Teresa could feel herself starting to get agitated at the thought of their daughter's splendid ambition being added to the long list of things he considered inherently ridiculous: bank ads; Nora Ephron; chiropractic ("How do they use that as a noun? That's an *adjective*"); vanity plates.

But could a high school girl even attend such a thing? Plus, the whole business would cost plenty. Plus, if she was honest with herself, she also thought it was nuts.

Ruby resented any indication that her mother found her knowable. Teresa remembered, years earlier, an eight-year-old Ruby saying, "I don't know why, but if I read the word *wink*, I have to wink."

"Me, too," Teresa replied unthinkingly. "By now I'm just about able not to do it, if I try hard. It's almost a reflex, the way that eye wants to close."

Ruby had been surprised, then disbelieving, then furious. "You do not! You do not! I'm not just copying you," she raged. She was unconsoled when Teresa said that people were very much like one another, that idiosyncrasies were shared, were handed down, were widespread among large groups. It was the first time Teresa had seen Ruby craving a privacy that included her thoughts.

Ruby was of course not her mother repeated; still, a lot of what Teresa knew about her daughter was gleaned through observation sharpened by self-knowledge. She'd learned to keep quiet about this.

Ruby's latest discovery: topping out ceremonies, when the highest beam was put into place on a construction project. A spruce or fir was sometimes placed up there, as if it were Christmas; flags were raised, and there was food. Ruby showed her some examples, and Teresa agreed that it was a charming custom.

"This is nifty," she said.

"Look, here's another one," Ruby said, clicking over to a partially completed building in Norway.

"Yeah; I've never seen those before," Teresa said. "What is it you like about it?"

"Oh, Mom. Don't ask me a bunch of questions," Ruby said. "I don't know. The idea of all these workers having a party and being so proud of their building, I guess?"

The fulcrum of Ruby's current hobby was her interest in Rem Koolhaas, the Dutch architect. Like the larger arena of architecture itself, the keen focus on him had developed for mysterious, possibly arbitrary reasons. His company, the Office for Metropolitan Architecture, became a talking point in their household. Teresa heard about OMA's innovative philosophy, like discussing the needs of homeless users in planning the design of a library. These lectures could leave Teresa faintly embarrassed on her daughter's behalf; the way Ruby spoke about "Rem," as if she knew him, and his "firm," sounded so play-acting, such a reach. But whatever.

Ruby showed her photos. "That's Rem and Zaha. They worked together some in the early days, before she started her own firm."

"Zaha?"

"Zaha Hadid."

"Oh, that sounds familiar. Now, did she do the Vietnam memorial in Washington? Is that right?"

Ruby said, "I don't know. What's that?" She looked it up. "Mom, no. Good grief. That's somebody named Maya Lin. You're as bad as Dad."

"I don't think so," Teresa said.

"Last week he mixed up Elon Musk with Jamie Oliver."

Teresa said, "Well, there you go. I don't even think they look alike."

Ruby saw links and commonalities between her parents that Teresa knew had long since dissolved. That particular moon had waxed, waned, grown dark.

That evening Teresa read a bit about Zaha Hadid. Ah. She had seen one or two of these. That Aquatics Centre, like a stingray. A building reminiscent of a Petro-Can station; another like a stretched wad of pizza dough. This was not a bad thing for Ruby to be into.

Teresa and her work buddy, Walker, alternated bringing each other surprises from the bakery on Mondays, to power them past the start of the week. This morning Walker had brought prosciutto croissants, so unexpectedly heavy with fat that when he handed her the bag she dropped it. Pastry flakes sprayed across her desk.

"We won't be hungry till dinnertime," she said.

"They're insane," Walker agreed, setting his own bag on a paper towel with an audible thump. "Thing probably weighs a pound. How was the weekend?"

"Good. Usual." She reached behind her to crank up the space heater they shared; their trailer was cold, and she and Walker drank a lot of instant coffee. "How was yours?"

"Game Saturday; game yesterday."

"Ugh; poor you," she said. His daughter Allegra played competitive hockey, so Walker and his wife, Heather, dutifully shivered through tournaments on their squashy foam cushions in the stands. Walker tried not to complain about it around his family and griped to Teresa instead.

"Anything new with Ruby?" he asked. There was usually something.

"Ruby wants to go to an architecture conference, in Toronto, by herself."

"What would she even do at a thing like that?"

"God, who knows. I think she just wants the experience of feeling like a grownup and wandering around on her own, but who can tell how her mind works. She's genuinely interested in the buildings, which is nice to see. She'd probably make a good architect."

"So, does she get to go to Toronto alone?"

She shot him a flat look. "No."

Teresa and Walker worked for a company that did soil analysis and amelioration for cropland. There were six employees—four with office space in the renovated bungalow that was the company headquarters, and the two of them outside in their small trailer, handling research needed for upcoming projects and follow-up on the projects they were finishing. Walker had worked there several years longer than Teresa, and when she was hired she didn't recognize him at first. He hadn't been bald in high school, when they wasted time goofing off during art club and on school orchestra trips.

He'd become a friend again over the past six years. During and following her divorce, he always struck the right note of support without curiosity. Now they swapped notes on their daily lives, but never too much.

Ruby had expressed concern that her mom and Walker might get together.

"Rube, in the first place, I'm not attracted to him. Okay? At all. And I can't see that ever changing. In the second place, he's got a wife, and I think he's pretty happy with her. And in the third place. . . ." She cast her mind around. "Having him as a work friend, a person I can talk about stuff with, means I don't really get lonely so much, which means I'm far less likely to start dating some unsuitable guy just to keep me company. All right? That means my being buddies with Walker helps keep our family the way it is, which is the way I like it and, I think, the way you do too, for now." *Good speech*, she congratulated herself. Also true, which always helped.

Ruby brightened. "Really? There's not anything between you? You're sure? And there's not going to be?"

"Really. We're not going to see each other outside work, and we're certainly not going to lock the trailer and get personal in there. So you can be polite when you come to the office without worrying that he's going to abandon Heather and move in here, and that you'll have to share a room with Allegra."

"Mom! I wasn't wondering about that." Teresa, who hadn't actually thought Ruby was concerned about such a scenario, saw by that sudden closed-door expression that it was precisely what she had been imagining.

The beauty of Walker was that he remembered Teresa as she used to be, but only vaguely. Their friendship had been a diffuse, crowd-based thing, with no special attachments or fierce loyalty. Each of them had long since forgotten anything embarrassing the other had done or been during high school, and only benign and harmless memories remained.

One day he reminded Teresa how much she had loved James Bond. He said, "You and Tara Therriault were always reading those books in chemistry lab."

"That's right," Teresa said. "I wonder when we stopped reading those." How long had it lasted? A year? She and Tara had read their way through James's exploits in strict order, memorizing arcane details of watches, guns, restaurant menus, engines, and high-stakes card games. What she'd admired most was his competence. She could so clearly recall her amorphous longing toward James, a desire both to marry him and to be him.

She was his age now, she realized, startled. And she'd neither married him nor turned into him; but, writing up a soil acidity test result, she could still dimly feel that ambition to become Bond, alone in a car, downshifting for a sharp turn on the hills above Monaco.

In scouting the web for Koolhaas-related footage, Ruby came across a video that showed the two towers of the

CCTV building, in Beijing, being joined. It had been done in midair, and Ruby explained to Teresa some of the constraints the engineers had faced.

"They had to do it at dawn, Mom; otherwise one part would have been hotter, because of the sun, and that would have thrown off their calculations. And it had to be a still day, not windy. It came down to millimetres." She showed Teresa a mid-project photo of the cantilevered extensions reaching longingly toward each other, like two bridges of Avignon trying to reunite.

"Neat," Teresa said; and it was neat. "I wonder how high up that is. That connecting part."

"That's the Overhang," Ruby answered, from her irritatingly complete body of knowledge. "It starts after the thirty-sixth floor and goes up thirteen floors above that. At the big moment when they were ready to join, and the two parts met, they just locked seven bolts in place, and it was done." Her sign was gusty. "I wish I'd been there to see it. I wish I'd been interested in buildings then."

As if she could simply have requested a trip to China to view a tightly regulated event, one not open to the public. Teresa tried to imagine some process through which she and Ruby might have gained access and materialized there, a random Canadian woman with no knowledge of skyscraper construction, with her seemingly even-more-random daughter, peering up into the sky while this engineering miracle took place far above them.

Ruby added, "Because it couldn't be done. Or lots of people thought it couldn't, and no one was sure what would happen."

"Was there any sort of backup plan?" Teresa asked, but Ruby didn't know that.

It stuck with Teresa for days—how linking the towers in midair had meant accomplishing the thing that couldn't be done. That investment in the chance of a favourable outcome. And the possibility of failure, like a net beneath them that would catch them and be not that bad.

It was Walker who came across the event.

"Check this out," he said one afternoon in their chilly trailer, emailing her a link. It was for a conference in Quebec City on the role of green spaces in community planning. Several of the English-language talks would be at the fine arts museum, in the new addition that had been an OMA project.

"I bet we could persuade Ralph to send you, and you could take Ruby along," Walker said.

"Are you nuts? This has zero overlap with what we do. Ralph would never agree."

"Sure he would. We can both work on him," Walker said. "Why wouldn't he agree? It's been a good year. Tell him this is relevant if he wants to expand more into urban areas. They should be priming their green spaces appropriately before investing in new projects; it's right up our alley."

"You think? That's awfully tenuous."

"Use the word 'because' when you lay out your case. The *Harvard Business Review* says that's persuasive, even with a bullshit argument."

It was persuasive. Teresa was starting to believe it herself, and she knew it was nonsense. "You're right," she said. "I haven't been anywhere for work in, what, three years, and that was just down to Guelph. We're overdue for some current insights in this place."

"Exactly. Ralph should be thinking more strategically about the future."

The revelatory joy of the conference came at the registration table, when they discovered Ruby had been registered alongside Teresa as a participant.

"Why did I get included?" Ruby whispered. "I thought I'd just be hanging around in the halls a lot."

"Maybe Ralph got you registered with a student discount? I guess?" Teresa suggested. "It was a really nice thing to do."

Ruby was admiring the folio she'd been handed and peering into her bag of loot. "Look at all this *stuff*," she said, clicking the end of a weighty pen. "Look, this magnet is a little pot of grass."

The best part for Ruby, though, was exploring the building. She gave rapt attention to the angles of the white beams along the glass walls; the elongated curves of a staircase; the airy, elegant restaurant, which she was afraid to get too close to. "I'm afraid they'll look at me," she muttered, nudging her mom back toward the less-scary side of the large foyer, where the gift shop was.

Teresa was quite taken with a golden wall that was an elevator, an expanse of brass buffed down to a dim shine and indistinct reflections, like a mirror that had lost its usefulness. Though it was utterly plain and unembellished, the colour of the metal seemed to promise mid-century glamour and some sort of retro hijinks, as if the doors were about to slide open to reveal, say, Zsa Zsa Gabor in a plunging neckline at a birthday fête.

"I would live in here," Teresa said. "Right in this elevator. It would be my own little apartment."

A few months after their Quebec City conference, Ruby came to tell Teresa she'd tracked down a site that would be livestreaming the Pritzker Prize ceremony from Berlin. Ruby wanted them both to get up at four in the morning to watch.

"I can tell you about the various projects and the different firms," Ruby said.

Parenting, Teresa thought, included so much time spent concealing reluctance, dismay, or a wish to bail.

"I'll make your coffee and take care of breakfast," Ruby offered, meaning she'd put the pod in the Keurig and the freezer waffles in the toaster, but it was well intentioned. She seemed excited about the prospect of an early-morning viewing.

"You watch without me," Teresa suggested. "Fill me in on it later."

"Mom, that's no fun. I don't even want to get up for it if you're not going to get up with me."

Well. This was probably worth it, then. What a change. Though when Teresa hauled herself from bed that morning, urged on by a beaming Ruby carrying a cup of coffee, she made her bleary way to the living room sofa for all the overseas prize excitement and was confronted by footage of an empty stage.

"Ruby, it's not even on! Why are we up? Do you know when this starts?"

"Mom, we'll get to see the whole thing. Look, I'll put the blanket on your feet. You can close your eyes if you want to."

"Why are we doing this?"

"Because it's *fun*," Ruby said.

Teresa dozed, and when she woke up Ruby was setting two plates of waffles on the coffee table. "They're starting," Ruby said, but there was still chair-moving, adjusting the microphone, waiting while people in Germany, where it was a decent hour, filtered into the room and the seats began to fill.

Teresa savoured the warmth of her coffee mug against her palms. She asked, "Are you still thinking you hope to become an architect?"

Ruby stared at her. "No. Why?"

"You're losing interest, you think? Considering other careers?"

"I've never wanted to be an architect."

"What? What are you talking about? What's the past year been about?"

"Not becoming an architect. Is that what you thought?"

"Well, yeah," Teresa said. "I mean. . . ."

"Is that the only reason you tried to be nice about it? Because you wanted me to do that?"

"I thought it was your goal. Your dad did, too. That's why he paid for you attend the conference in Quebec, so you'd have a better chance to study the building."

"I didn't know Dad paid! I thought Ralph paid for me, like he paid for you! Did Dad spend too much?"

"Ruby, don't get all worked up."

"How much did it cost? Was it too much money?"

"It's fine, no; it's fine. I found out after we got back sometime. He did it to surprise you, because he thought, we both did, that it was your career goal."

"Is that what you want? You want me to be an architect? Are you going to be disappointed in me if I don't decide to do that?"

"God, Ruby, no! I don't care what you decide to do; that's up to you. I just thought that was your direction."

"Because I don't think I could."

"Wasn't that what you've been planning all this time? To do when you grow up?"

"No, not at all. You can just like things. I like Harry Potter, but I don't want to be a wizard."

So. Maybe it wasn't the buildings Ruby was so drawn to, but innovation, newness, change. Or perhaps it was about being creative and having agency. Being in charge. Maybe she envied the sureness, the ability to bring projects to fruition.

Or possibly she was attracted to the idea of people who thoroughly enjoyed their careers. Not like a soil analyst and a family practitioner whose job hadn't ended up being quite what he pictured.

They ate their waffles on the sofa, with ramekins of syrup for dipping and their plates held below their chins to avoid drips. This was one of Teresa's shortcomings as a parent: a slack inattention, whenever possible, to the need for knives and forks.

"Is Dad going to be disappointed in me if he finds out that's not what I really want to do?"

"No, I don't think so, honey," Teresa answered. "He was happy to help you, or do what he thought was helpful, but he's not set on the idea. He and I were wondering, though—what got you interested in architecture in the first place?"

"I had to do a project at school on a public building, and I picked the Seattle library. Ms. Pelletier had a list we chose from. And that's an OMA building. You don't remember when I worked on it? I liked that building, and then I found out I liked other buildings, too, and it just became a thing. Here, we need to watch; they're really starting now."

For a card for Ruby's fifteenth birthday, Teresa laboriously tracked down a photo of the joining of the Beijing CCTV towers. She was able to find a scene shot from up at the Overhang, where the seven bolts were about to be snapped into place, with some specks that could be people visible on the ground far below. She picked out two dots to represent her and Ruby, and drew an arrow pointing to them. *Look*, she wrote beside it. *Here we are*.

Why had she assumed architecture was Ruby's career goal? Partly, Teresa thought, because it was such a reflexive inquiry for adults to pester kids with, this *What do you want to be when you grow up* business. But part of it was on her, getting sucked into a simplistic assumption without nuance, without questions; she had been oblivious of complexity. As if Ruby were an idle acquaintance, rather than the person deserving of Teresa's finest, most granular attention. Her care.

A bit later, Teresa would wonder whether one function of Ruby's interest in buildings and Rem Koolhaas and OMA had been to provide a focus for her admiration—an area that she'd deemed, on her own, to be worthy and solid. Though her daughter generally behaved respectfully toward people, Teresa got the sense that Ruby had an uneasy relationship with her own rearing contempt, trying to stuff it down and keep it from getting out of hand. Watching Ruby, Teresa found she could remember the pulse of her own high-school years, how she and her friends used to alternate between fiery scorn and regret that they were being mean. (No one had been safe from their scathing judgment, which was based mainly on disappointment and got divided impartially among parents, teachers, classmates, relatives, famous people, and passersby.) Perhaps Ruby had found herself pinched in that same uncomfortable trap. Here, though, in these ambitious structures, in the craggy and avuncular face shown in the photos of Rem Koolhaas, and in the careful work of his partners on their projects across the globe, she had identified an appropriate channel for her enthusiasm. Here was something that merited her meticulous alertness, untainted by scorn, still enviable. Her devotion had been an edifice she created, on her own. What a relief it must have been to her, finding an outlet both real and remote, a safe place for all that fierce love to land.

Volunteer

Trap-Neuter-Release was how I ended up at a November event at the unprosperous local mall, staffing a red-and-green table where people could sign up to sponsor a neutering. Fun gift. Important, though, and I tried to convey to people who stopped how much good they would be doing by helping us out. I had all the statistics at hand on bird deaths. (Cats kill a crazy number of birds; I've learned all this stuff. Power lines and wind farms are not the problem—it's Smoke and Pumpkin doing all the damage.) And, since people like local, I tried to keep my explanations as specific to Ontario as possible.

The young woman staffing the table with me wore a Jughead-style jingle bell hat over her long, pale brown hair, and she took it off and shook it at passing children in time to the carols, as if it were a tambourine. She kept poking cat treats into the carriers of the ribbon-bedecked hopefuls we had brought with us to charm shoppers. "Gather round, kitties," she'd say, pushing more nuggets through their wires. "Gotta keep your strength up for this big bad world."

"Don't you think they've had enough treats?" I said.

"They're putting up with a lot, coping with all this racket today," she said. "One afternoon in a food coma won't hurt them, and at least they'll get some enjoyment out of being on display like this."

I don't know why I thought she'd listen to me, except that I'm twenty-five years older and listening seems like the thing women do, especially when the other person has politely prefaced a comment with "don't you think."

I felt uncomfortably on display myself, the way you can when you're trying to get strangers to participate in something worthwhile. Still, the cats' sweet faces were extraordinarily appealing; we got some adoption requests.

"Fill out a form, and we'll drop it off at the shelter," I'd say. "If these guys are still available after your application is approved, you're welcome to request a particular one." The SPCA has gotten more stringent than people expect.

But most shoppers didn't want to talk to us, cute cats notwithstanding; three-quarters of the passersby would look at our table with cautious interest, but if we made eye contact they were gone.

Katelyn, my partner for the afternoon, liked to jitter and bop around and engage with people. I'm more the sitting-still type. She did a few table push-ups.

"You should have brought your dog," she said.

"Was I telling you about him?" Sometimes I'm concerned about dementia.

"No, but I remember him. Archie?"

"You know him? From where?"

"You live next door to Cheryl, right? I used to help her make candy kebabs to sell at the farmers' market."

"Oh, I remember that," I said. "You made them out on her screened porch." I'd be out back weeding; I'd seen Katelyn a few times. But it was weird that she hadn't told me who she was when we arrived to do our setup. Her chatting and her air of breeziness didn't seem like someone who'd just not mention, oh, by the way, we sort of know each other.

"You didn't recognize me, right?" she asked, and I realized what she might be thinking. Because both of us are heavier than we used to be. I'd already thought we looked uncomfortably like a matched set there at our adoption table—two white pears in red sweaters. But of course it's not as if encountering heavy people is a rare thing. That self-conscious feeling of exposure is mostly all in your head. I'm not saying other people don't immediately see me as fat, and rarely anything else; they aren't studying how well I execute every tiny act, though. Ordinary life isn't a complicated performance like some Roger de Coverley line dance where you might screw up literally at any second.

I spoke to her as if not wanting to wound my own younger self. "Your hair is different, and I don't think you wore makeup then," I said. She now wore eyeshadow and winged eyeliner, quite striking. Her blouse was cut to skim over the rolls around her middle. I recognized her size and knew how that body feels. I'm like the drawing of the "one weird tip" internet ad, the one where the person is grabbing two handfuls of belly like a loaf of bread. Not that I want liposuction or anything, but I can understand the urge, because sometimes the fat seems so discrete. You can hoist it up in a bundle and think, Now if I could just have this pooch taken off.

Ah, well.

"I haven't seen Cheryl in a long time," she said. "She was my Scout leader back in middle school. I know she liked you. She used to talk about you sometimes."

"Oh? What did she say?"

"I can't remember. That you were a good cook. That you'd never been married. Stuff like that. She said you were nice."

"She said I'd never been *married*?"

"Yeah; why? Are you?"

"No, no. She's right—I've never been married. But I was in a relationship for nearly twenty years, so it wasn't that different," I said.

"Oh. Was that before you met her?"

"No, it was while I lived next door to her. With Conrad."

"So Cheryl never met him?"

What; she thought I'd kept him hidden? I said, "No, you don't understand—he lived with me, Katelyn. We were Cheryl's neighbours for—fifteen years? Conrad made ketchup with her one summer. He helped her turn her compost."

I couldn't imagine what Cheryl had been thinking, talking about me this way. As if Conrad and I had been some half-rate couple from a clearance shelf, because she had a document that I didn't have but also didn't want.

Maybe she hadn't been talking about us, though; perhaps she'd been speaking about the institution of marriage itself. Maybe she even envied me. It wasn't sounding like that, but perhaps the way Katelyn told it, and the way I heard it, were both different from what Cheryl had meant.

I thought about that on the drive home—we had gotten four neutering sponsorships done, not a great return on two people spending a holiday-season Saturday afternoon at the mall, but also not a bad outcome—and swung my car into my driveway, looking over at Cheryl's small lighted house. I wondered what people thought of my choices. Did other women assume my life hadn't started yet?

Before I opened my car door, I could already hear Archimedes barking his little lungs out in disbelieving joy.

Archie doesn't run errands anymore, due to the likelihood that some overly fanatic passerby will see him alone in the car and call the RCMP on me, or just break the window and confiscate him, regardless of the mildness of the day. The whole thing is a shame, because going on errands is his purpose in life. My favourite thing about dogs is their busy attention to their work, and when they're kept from it, or limited in the scope of their duties, you can tell by their faces that it diminishes them.

So that wish to find Archie somewhere new to hang out was what got me involved with the SPCA. I thought it might be an opportunity for him to come somewhere dog-friendly with me, do some dog socializing, and we'd be contributing to the community together.

They needed walkers, all right. Most of those dogs are frantic to get outside—it feels as if you come back from even a short jaunt with your leash-holding arm longer than the other one. The SPCA reminds me of a nursing home, in that it sounds like such a swell arrangement—all those new friends, and the place is run

by professionals who have your best interests at heart!—
when instead most of the occupants look pretty miserable.

And in fact Archimedes was awful there; the bonds I
thought might happen between him and the less-lucky
dogs didn't materialize. Rather than looking pleased
about having a new companion on our walk, he looked
pissed. By then I'd seen, though, how useful I was to
the beleaguered shelter staff, so I began coming twice a
week to do some rounds. Back home I'd give privileged
Archie a belly rub, and I always had that feeling you get,
when they sniff your legs in their canny way, that he
could tell exactly what kinds of dogs I'd been cheating
on him with.

And the cats! So many. That got me involved with
their Trap-Neuter-Release program, where stray cats
aren't trapped for adoption but only for sterilizing in
order to live out their wild lives and finally die on their
own terms, without replacing themselves several hundred times over.

Of course, they kill lots of birds in their extra years.

Some things have no good solution.

When I was young and not yet heavy, my looks weren't
something I devoted a lot of energy to. I wasn't a sen-
sation, but I was pretty enough. To me, being beautiful
just seemed like another way of feeling loved: It might
have been nice, but I didn't think I needed it—I was
already loved.

Why did I imagine my desirability would last?
Because, I suppose, I thought it was inherent in me.
All the men who'd wanted me, who in my twenties had
asked me out at parties or approached me in bars or got-

ten my phone number at inter-office softball games—each of those a lovely thing that only happened once or twice, but those times were enough—I assumed those men were drawn by something that was part of me and would never go away. My worth.

But did they see nothing but my cuteness? My undeniably average and yet sufficient cuteness. Was that the total of what I'd had to offer, after all—a shy sparkle? Evidently it trickled away during all those years I was with Conrad, like a gift card forgotten in the junk drawer, worthless by the time you need it again. I wasn't paying attention. And this diminution, so invisible to me, had ramifications now, the major one being that apparently my dating days were over.

I'd realized our couplehood would mean fidelity and monogamy. I didn't know there was a risk my ability to attract new partners would leach away without my knowledge. And here's Conrad, with his beard trimmed (it no longer looks messy and as if you might notice crumbs in it), inexplicably turning him handsome. Even his baldness suits him these days, with his formerly pelt-like hair now cropped to a silver band that looks like money. He runs around town in those J. Crew shirts you see all over; when the hell has Conrad ever worn J. Crew? Never, that's when.

Whereas over the decades I've gained sixty pounds, every ounce of it around my middle.

The following week Katelyn and I were back by the Cinnabon, this time with only two cat hopefuls. I got there early and finished my Christmas shopping at the bookstore; I like to be done, ideally, before the start of December. This would be my third Christmas since

Conrad and I ended things, and being single definitely streamlined the prep work.

When I reached our table spot, Katelyn had set us up with a cat carrier at each end; those silent tan and white paws with their pink-bean pads kept emerging from narrow slots, groping around on the tabletop, and soundlessly retracting. Once again we weren't busy. Our table created a lacuna in the mid-mall space—most shoppers swerved around us while gazing away, preferring even shuttered stores. Here's who seemed to want to talk to us: the desperate; the lonely; the animal lovers; the unusually outgoing or confident. Also children. The Santa Land area had been set up but wouldn't be staffed for another week; so far there were only penguins gliding on a silver pond and slowly waving polar bears flanking a vacant throne with a butt-dented green seat cushion.

We took turns going for lunch at Monica's Spot, a sole-proprietor café down at one end of the lean food court.

"This mall's getting sad," I said, when I returned.

"It's gone downhill a lot from when I was little," she said. But before we left that afternoon, we got another neutering sponsorship, and three more families filled out adoption papers.

One of the things she'd thought would be fun at the shelter, Katelyn told me, was choosing names for the animals that came in. "I guess everybody thinks it's really cool at first. That's what they tell me. Then you name twenty or thirty cats and stop caring about matching their names with their personalities—just Lola, Doris, whatever."

"Doris Whatever is a great name for a tabby," I said.

"See? You would totally get into it. Plus you can name all the evil-tempered ones after your enemies. Volunteer for the a.m. shift, when all the activity happens." Katelyn was taking a year off from finishing her culinary skills diploma at community college, and her parents wanted her to do more than hang around the house cooking, she said.

Tempting as it sounded, though, to spend my mornings naming kittens and maybe giving them milk from a baby bottle, I work in the daytime, in the office at Stannus Toyota. I like my job and the crew at work, even though I'm not exactly making use of my degree in German. I don't love scheduling transmission repairs and logging our parts deliveries, but there's more to it than you might think.

Katelyn's mother had been dead set against her volunteering. "She's afraid I'll get bitten by a dog that's been damaged," she said. "My mom has a friend whose daughter got bitten on the face, and she has some pretty dramatic scars."

"Yeah, that's something to be wary about, all right," I said, never having given any thought to what it might be like to have a dog bite your face. Even thinking about it a little, once I let myself envision it, was terrifying. "So what did you tell her?"

She shrugged. "Just that, you know, she doesn't get to make all my decisions anymore. She's also worried I'll get toxoplasmosis there."

"What's that?" I asked.

"You know. That cat disease."

I had no idea what she meant.

"You get it from cats that have been in the wild, or that are sick," she said.

"From being bitten? Or scratched?"

"No, I don't think so. From changing litter, from the poop. It's a bacteria, I think. A parasite? Is that different from bacteria?"

"Uh, I think those are bigger, but I'm not sure," I said. One-celled organisms; were some of those parasites? "Does it make you really sick?"

While she was telling me about it, my CBC listening came back to me. Toxoplasmosis changes behaviour by altering brain chemistry in profound and lasting ways. The parasite is able to influence the host's behaviour, making people more inclined to take unusual risks. It has disturbing effects on personality, on decision-making, on relationships. I watched those cat legs silently dabbing the area of the tabletop they could reach through their openings, and they looked less imploring and benign. Shouldn't the SPCA folks have reminded me of this possibility when I dropped in to volunteer?

I told Katelyn, "Well, your mom's smart to be worried. I mean, it's real, right? The link isn't imagined?"

She shrugged. "No, it's real. I mean, I guess. It was all over the news and online last year. Didn't you see it?"

"Yeah, I did," I said. "I just forgot it, because I don't have a cat. Dogs don't get it? Just cats?"

"Yeah, I mean, I think," she said. "Anyway, my mom freaked out and didn't want me to volunteer with the organization at all. I had to promise her I wouldn't clean any litter boxes there, under any circumstances. I said, 'God, Mom, choose something a little more realistic to worry about.'"

I thought that actually her mom's worries were pretty smart. "This was linked to car accidents; am I remembering that right? Because of the risk-taking behaviour. And, was it suicides?"

"That's right. And people cheating on their spouses; that was a big thing."

"Well, doesn't all that bother you? Do you believe it?"

"Yeah; not really," she said. "Or I believe it but I'm not concerned. I guess I just think we have bigger things to worry about, you know?"

"No," I said.

"Well, like, if this is so common, and it's been around for so long, isn't it kind of already integrated into our behaviour patterns? So that, as a society, we're already coping with it?"

"Yeah; I don't think it works like that," I said. "If the link hasn't been definitively proven, I guess it could be all a mistake. But from what I remember, there was credible evidence."

Katelyn said vaguely, "Well, maybe. It just sounds like one of those big shocking possibilities there's no point in worrying about. Take a chance, you know?"

"So you're not so risk-averse," I said. She's got toxoplasmosis already, I thought, but I had the good manners not to say that.

Wednesday evening I got caught in that midweek funk that comes sometimes. Everything can feel different in the evening, of course. Looking at my bags of presents to wrap, proofing yeast for the cinnamon coffee cakes I planned to bake, my life seemed utterly predictable. Not that I wanted to get a feces-borne life-altering disease and have my decision-making driven by the unthinking biological needs of a parasite I was harbouring. I mean, obviously. It was just that Katelyn's blasé attitude, even though I thought it was wrong-headed and foolish, also had some appeal for me.

Thursday I got a call from Christine at the SPCA. The holiday season was proving fruitful in terms of kitten adoption as well as our cheerless gifts of feline neutering; could the two of us manage a few more Saturdays?

"But discourage adopting on impulse, of course," she said; unplanned pet purchases are the bane of SPCAs everywhere—all those aging backyard chickens and bitey hedgehogs, dropped off at shelters so the householders can feel free again.

"Don't feel obligated," Christine told me belatedly, when I'd already said yes. Katelyn and I had managed to get Dusty, Chess, Moonshine, and Fleur placed in new homes, a development that gave me an unanticipated level of satisfaction. Those shelter cages are just so small.

That next Saturday the Santa Land photo corner was open, so there were plenty of kids for Katelyn to shake her jingle hat at. Again we took turns going for lunch at the sandwich kiosk, Monica's, which I hoped would be busier today.

"Did you see her little signs?" Katelyn asked, when I returned. These were a new addition—six or eight, hand-lettered on pieces of posterboard.

"Oh, my god," I said. "So beseeching. 'Have you tried our chicken salad?' 'Our decadent chocolate cake is homemade!'"

"I nearly cried," Katelyn said. "Thinking of her at home, carefully lettering them."

"Cutting them out. Making those cloud shapes."

"Putting them on top of her bag so she wouldn't forget to bring them in the morning," she said. "Just tragic."

"Or heroic," I said. "Isn't she heroic for persisting? Maybe? Yes?"

"Maybe, but it still breaks my heart," she said. "She watches you walk toward the booth, and she looks so hopeful. This isn't making fun of her, is it? Are we being mean?"

I shook my head. "It's more like the opposite of making fun of her. We're supporting her from afar. Bearing witness."

"To her struggle," Katelyn said. "This is why I had to stop working at the farmer's market; I couldn't handle seeing all the transactions."

"I know exactly," I said. "I can't buy my produce from someone who wants the sale so much. What if you choose the next stand, instead? It's crippling."

A young couple with a toddler spotted Katelyn and approached our table, waving greetings.

"This is my cousin Eric; and his wife, Jordan; and Caleb," she introduced us, putting her hat on Caleb, who was gazing, entranced, at our cats of the day. "This is my friend Molly," she told them, and I felt a ridiculous rush of pleasure at being described that way; we'd spent maybe eight hours together.

Yet that week I'd thought of things I would mention on Saturday. I was wearing a sweater I thought was cool.

It's not the admiration that's embarrassing, I concluded; articulating it makes it pitiful. I dislike looking foolish, even in the mirror. Better, sometimes, not to peer too closely at what I'm thinking.

The straightforward emotions—envy, anger, fear— it's easy to imagine other people feeling those. The more whorled and nuanced motivations, though, are impossible for me to attribute to anyone else. Do people ever get dressed and hope I'll admire that outfit? And why is it that I so want compliments from people who are such a small part of my life?

Another neutering sponsorship was completed before Katelyn and I wrapped up that day. And her cousin and his wife applied to adopt Mocha, so Caleb could grow up with a cat and not develop allergies. A taxi driver who wanted company since his daughter had left for university filled out an application for Strawberry, and two different families wanted Pearl. "Read up on toxoplasmosis!" I said. "Don't get sick!"

The following Saturday we were handed Belle, as well as a withdrawn, nameless fluffball. We tossed around ideas on the way over. Gertie? April?

"Let's call her Monica," I suggested.

Katelyn poked a gentle fingertip in the carrier and said, "Hello, Monica." The kitten quivered for a long moment, but at last she approached. Her cautious nose. So brave.

Dogs That Rest Their Heads

"I'd say 'potential son-in-law' is more accurate than 'future son-in-law,'" Warren said. "I haven't seen her jump up and down about planning any wedding. Going on vacation with her girlfriends. She loves that dog a lot more than she loves Toby, if you ask me."

"Well, he's not that bad," Eleanor said. "I know he gets on your nerves, but how much did my dad like spending time with you when we were dating?"

"True enough," said Warren.

"If you'd make more effort." But she said it mildly. She was working at the stove, with her back toward him. Warren turned over a couple of lettuce leaves in the blue plastic salad bowl, looking for red pepper slices. "Don't nose around in there, Warren; I'm nearly done. Can you get the water?"

"Anyway, I make plenty of effort with him," Warren said. "It's nothing but effort, when they're here." He got down two glasses and thought back to some of Lindsay's boyfriends that he'd actually liked. There was that Greg, who played cards and even talked Lindsay into playing. And Patrick something, Peter, who told him about Merrell shoes, so great that for ten or twelve years Warren had worn almost no other kind. Long gone, but his shoe guidance lasted. And aside from Warren's own level of comfort with those two and the others like them, the better boyfriends, Lindsay had clearly cared a lot for them. The lilt in her voice over this guy or that one used to embarrass him, make him helplessly change the subject, as if he'd opened the bathroom door at the wrong moment.

Toby was fine; there was nothing wrong with him. He and Lindsay had been together for probably five or six years now, so of course those headiest first days were behind them. To be expected. Warren's only difficulty, really, was that he had to keep trying to warm to him. That earnestness.

Toby volunteered at an animal shelter on Saturdays—laudable, obviously—and once he and Warren had been discussing dogs. Warren mentioned that only well into adulthood had he realized how many breeds rested their heads on the side of their beds, or on some convenient person's ankle. "I always thought it was just this idiosyncrasy my own dogs had," he said.

Toby smiled. "Yeah, it's a thing a lot of breeds do," he said. Then he said that, at the shelter, they used the word "who" rather than "that." Warren hadn't even understood what he was talking about. Warren's idea in telling the story—if he had had a reason, which he hadn't, he'd just been making conversation—was to say, *Look, kid, I'm not always that bright.* Connecting through self-deprecation.

"We would say, 'dogs who rest their heads,'" Toby clarified. "Instead of 'dogs that rest their heads.' At first it sounded strange to me, but not anymore. It's a way of respecting the dog, like you would a person."

"Well, now," Warren said, which meant a sharp glance from Eleanor and an internal ping of thankfulness that Lindsay was downstairs, poking around in the basement, out of hearing. For both their sakes.

Lindsay and Toby were both in their mid-thirties, so it made sense that Toby wasn't one of the intimidated youth of the past. Warren himself was getting older, though, at a rate that kept the gap from closing for him. He used to be middle aged, and they were all young.

"We're getting old, babe," he said to Eleanor a few times a year, and somehow it was always truer than before. Grace Slick had turned 75. Stevie Nicks, 70; Bill Wyman, 80. Beyond comprehension.

Perhaps, at heart, he thought Toby simply wasn't good enough for Lindsay. His outdoorseyness must have been part of the appeal—Toby had studied geology, which was proving not to be all that useful in the resource-economy downturn—and they both liked demanding sports. Paddle boarding. Mountain biking. Lindsay was tougher than either of her parents, Warren had long believed, though perhaps it was the job of the father to think that about his girl—an unspoken requirement he'd absorbed without realizing it was part of the deal. He remembered a couple of soccer game pictures in the paper when she was in high school, how she'd been photographed grimacing, straining forward, shirt askew, twisting away from a girl trying to cut her off. Strong as a German Shepherd. Warren trusted both his kids to take care of themselves, but David was more impulsive than Lindsay, less able to anticipate consequences. Lindsay had that planning, entrepreneurial streak; she'd sold cookies at the farmers' market. And, one Halloween, fancy pumpkin-carving templates that she'd made herself. Three dollars each—she'd come home with thirty-six dollars and been delighted. Twelve years old.

"El, when are they getting here?" he called from the den, where he was tidying the desk, feeding papers with satisfaction into the grinding, crunching teeth of the shredder. He appreciated its deliberate savagery at its job.

"Tomorrow, lunchtime," Eleanor said.

"And how long will they be here?"

"Four days. Then Lindsay's coming back later in the summer." Lindsay was a teacher and was finishing her second master's; her summers filled up fast, but he knew she came as often as she could.

"That's good," he said. "What do you want for dinner tomorrow? Or do you want to go out?"

"Fish, maybe? Potato salad?"

"Sure," he said. He remembered his mother, how she'd written out her potato salad recipe for Eleanor the first time they met, when he took her to his parents' house for a picnic. Now his mother's photo hung among a grouping over the desk, with her silver hair in a French roll and her final poodle, mean little Ouida, on her lap. She'd been a country girl who grew up sleeping three to a bed and assumed the effortless postwar expansion of the middle class was permanent.

He wondered how many dozens of times Eleanor had made that potato salad, something he'd never thought about before, and he realized you wouldn't need a recipe for it. A few ingredients, thrown in to taste; heavy on the salt. (His observation, in retirement: Take an old worn-out memory and reflect on it in a new context, and it might yield fresh wisdom.) His mother had probably written it on a recipe card—which women kept on hand, back then, stacks of blank ones at readiness—as a gesture of her welcoming kindness. El had been too inexperienced a cook to realize how simple it was.

He finished tidying the desk and wandered into the bathroom, where El was on the toilet. "Do you think you had a good relationship with my mother?"

She gave him an exasperated look. "Will you stop worrying? She can make her own choices. It's sort of not any of our business."

"I know. I certainly didn't think my parents' feelings had any bearing on who I dated."

She laughed. "I liked your mother fine. She got on my nerves sometimes, but she was so good to me, always. Could I have a little privacy?"

Warren had never had insomnia until he hit seventy, but now he often woke up at four or five. It had seemed to come on with his prostate troubles. Chasing sleep was worse than getting up. He made some of the vegetable soup Lindsay liked, to take back with her, and started a pot of coffee. Then he napped for a time in the big chair, and woke up when Eleanor came downstairs.

"Uh oh," she said. "You're still brooding."

"I don't want her to live the rest of her life with some know-it-all, street preacher-y type who has all the answers," Warren said. Toby had a disconcerting use of "that's because." Warren had once said the evening was hotter than the day, and Toby said, "That's because the wind dies down."

Eleanor said, "What, you want her to be with someone where she's calling all the shots? Making the decisions?"

"I guess so," Warren said. "If that's more likely to make her happy. Which common sense suggests it would."

"I don't think that would make her too happy," El said. "Fifty-fifty; that's the ticket. Or sixty-forty. You don't want to be with someone you boss around all the time."

"No," he said doubtfully. "No, that's true."

The next evening after dinner, he and Toby sat in the den watching television while Lindsay and her mother drove into town for some particular sorbet Lindsay had in mind. Ice skating wasn't Warren's first viewing choice—he'd suggested it because it was long—but undeniably there was something transfixing about the score announcements, the kiss-and-cry scenes, and the overkill of those fluttery winged costumes.

"They don't get dizzy at all, do they?" he offered, and Toby earned a point in Warren's estimation by not explaining how the skaters avoided vertigo. A girl in yellow spun out on her flip, landed on her knee, and bobbed up, wincing and smiling, to continue. One in purple and silver glided around the outside of the arena, lowered in a near-squat with her feet turned out, in a posture that always looked inexpressibly vulgar to Warren. He thought, but did not say, "She looks like she's about to dribble onto the ice." He could have said it to El, except that he'd said it before and she only found things funny the first time. He could have said it to Lindsay when she still lived at home, but perhaps not anymore.

After skating, they watched a few minutes of *Parking Wars*, until Warren felt he might have a stroke from boredom.

"Want to take the dog out for a quick stroll?" he suggested. Swan, Toby and Lindsay's fragile greyhound, clambered awkwardly to her feet. They went out the back door and wandered down to the barrier that marked the end of the road, then let her cautiously investigate some of the more benign-looking trash at the edge of the pavement.

As they headed back, Toby suggested, "You want to take her?"

"Sure," Warren said, surprised; he hadn't walked a dog in years. She was polite, not a puller, and the slight tension that travelled up the leash and along his arm reminded him pleasurably of how readily dogs communicated their wishes. Three or four minutes of walking Swan were enough to start him musing that maybe it would be nice to have a dog again. Toby looked pleased.

"She's a good girl," he said. She was, and Warren thought he could find his way to a more nuanced liking of Toby, if they spent more time together.

They ate raspberry sorbet and talked a while, filling Lindsay in on the neighbours' news and friends' illnesses, recoveries, and deaths. She updated them on her classes and coursework. Around ten they headed for bed. Warren could tell El was bothered by something.

"What's happened?" he asked her, when they were in their room with the door closed.

"Well," she said. "We went to Starbucks." Where they had talked.

Toby, it appeared, had been working part-time over the past year. He'd taken some courses to improve his job prospects, and he was job-hunting. And now he owed Lindsay something on the order of twenty-six thousand dollars.

"So they haven't merged their finances yet?" he asked Eleanor. "Maybe that's not such a bad sign. Maybe she's not too committed to him? Keeping things separate?"

Eleanor faltered, wanting to tell him something she was having trouble saying.

"Warren," she said, "I think she wants to leave him."

"I would, too," he said. "Anybody would! He's boring! Get the money back, and cut bait!"

"I don't think she will," Eleanor said.

"Why? What did you tell her? Shall I talk to her?"

"Maybe not yet," Eleanor said. "I think she won't leave him, even though she wants to. I think I'm understanding that right, Warren. That she would break up with him if the money weren't standing between them. But he can't pay her back, so she won't just go."

"You mean this debt is *tying* her to him? Like. . . against her will? She won't walk away from him because of this money?"

El didn't answer.

"That can't be right, can it? She's not stupid. God, El; why do you tell me these things."

"Calm down," she said. "I may have it wrong. She wasn't very forthcoming with me; I'm piecing together bits of what she explained while we were having coffee. But I think that's the situation."

This was the most pitiable thing Warren had heard in a long time, that his lovely daughter could be trapped by money owed to her. Money that no longer existed, that was gone; but maybe the hole, the negative balance, was clearer to Lindsay than the possibility of ending this thing and starting over somewhere else. The money wasn't real, but she couldn't let go of the knowledge that it should be.

If Toby wanted to keep her and had planned it all out in advance, Warren thought, he couldn't have come up with a more effective strategy. And yet it probably unspooled entirely by accident. What were the odds? The most foolproof and devious way to keep someone snared was also the most financially advantageous. And achieved without planning or forethought. It was ingenious—simple and invisible, a leash. If she let it be.

"I'll give her the money," Warren said. "If that's the only reason she's staying with him." Like the inverse of a dowry.

"I wish we could. But what about David? You can't give money like that to just one child. And we don't have an extra fifty-two thousand dollars."

"We won't tell David," Warren said. Eleanor gave him a look.

"Yet," he added. "We'll tell him later."

"Warren, make sense," she said. "We *cannot do that*. It is *not possible*. You know that."

"I'm sorry Toby was ever born," Warren said.

"I'm not sure about it; I told you, I'm guessing. I could be wrong. She wouldn't tell me outright, and I couldn't ask straight out."

"So she's hinting at this?"

Eleanor shook her head—not to say no, but to express dismayed confusion.

"You didn't know about this before, did you?" he asked her.

She said, "I suspected something. I could tell something was wrong there."

Warren's anger was not just toward Toby, but also toward Lindsay, for being stuck in this ludicrous and dignity-destroying situation; and even at Eleanor, for knowing—or semi-knowing—and not telling him earlier. He had the sense, for the good of his marriage, not to voice that he was perilously and illogically disgusted with his wife, and he knew that she could be directing similar thoughts toward him, for mysterious but internally logical reasons of her own.

"Is she hoping to get it back?" he asked Eleanor, and thought of gamblers at casino tables at four a.m. "Get him to repay it, then she'll leave him?"

"I don't know," El said. "I'm guessing, here. But I have a feeling she's going to marry him."

"Even though, you think, she'd really prefer to end it."

"Yeah. Even though."

That felt correct to Warren. Plausible and crazy and sad. His much-loved daughter, so tenacious and smart. But maybe this was all upside down, a misinterpretation. He tried to hold on to that possibility. He was going to have to live with a lot of ambiguity when it came to Toby, he could see. Forget ever growing close to the guy; instead, Warren would be stuck with decades of not knowing for certain whether he hated him or not.

His poor, caught daughter. Though he'd never talked to Lindsay about such a situation of debt, loss, and repayment, he would have hoped that he and El had shown her more than this about when to walk away. About priorities, and what to fix your life to. What mattered.

Maybe El had misheard, he thought, when he woke up at four and went to make coffee. With her hearing aids, and in a crowded coffee shop, she would have missed details. She might even be having some age-related confusion. A few times lately he'd wondered. This made him a little more sanguine. (Perhaps his only daughter's life hadn't foundered on the rocks! Maybe it was just his wife in the early stages of dementia!)

Still, he found he was counting steps, the old habit from the time after his father died, when Warren was fourteen, that still came back to him if he was troubled. It irritated him, but he'd learned over the decades not to try to muffle it. Steps to the table: six, seven, eight. Fridge, five, six, seven. Table again, three, four. His internal stress barometer.

He looked online, but selling his little boat would only bring in three or four thousand dollars. Not that he had hoped for a lot more, but the gap was despairing math. Pantry: twelve, thirteen, fourteen, fifteen. *Come on; stop it.* Trying to change it never did any good.

When his kids were little, of course he'd thought he would always be able to help them out. Certain times still pained him, when nothing he said seemed helpful. Like when Lindsay was being bullied about her nose.

This was different, a poor choice of her own making. Something she herself could set straight.

She needed to think in terms of amortizing the sunk costs, and how little that would amount to over the years to come. She had to be willing to walk away.

"Hi, you two," Warren said, when Lindsay and Toby came in with the dog. "You three." The dog yawned.

"Hi, Dad."

"Morning, Warren. You're up early."

Warren's hand, of its own volition, had already scooped the car key from its glass ashtray by the kitchen door.

"I'm just on my way out," he said. "Meeting Larry for breakfast."

He was down the road before he thought about where to go. Pick some strawberries, maybe. He stopped at the ATM for cash. "Exit screen?" it asked him. Warren punched the button to check the balances. Checking. Savings.

No, she would have to handle it herself. He withdrew a thousand dollars to give her. He would tell Eleanor after Lindsay and Toby left. For that matter, he thought, Eleanor might well do the same thing.

Warren was the second person at the U-pick place, and the young girl at the booth was too sleepy to direct him to a particular row. "Pick wherever," she said, waving a languid arm. "Just get them all, where you pick; don't leave red ones on the stems."

He knelt on the path. The berries were glossy red, half hidden. The boxes filled quickly, but Warren only picked three quarts and left.

Driving back, thinking of coffee, he saw Eleanor's

car at McDonald's. He swung in and parked beside her, then got in on the passenger's side.

"Here," she said, handing him her cup. "You can finish this."

"You don't want the rest of it? I can go inside."

"No, finish it. I had a cup at home."

He tasted cautiously; El used more cream than he liked.

"What are we doing today?" he asked.

"Well, they want to see a movie with us. So if there's anything you've been dying to see, it's a good time. Or maybe swim. You okay?"

"I'm okay," he said. "Fine. You?"

"Yeah, same," she said. "They'll make their own mistakes."

"True," he said. He knew she meant Lindsay and her brother; but, in a larger sense, also Toby. Also David's wife, Gretchen. Even Elsa, David and Gretchen's daughter, who was four and whose largest decisions involved which purple shirt to wear.

"I just hope she won't drift into getting married for some such damnfool reason," he said. A nail or staple of sadness inside him, some fastener that was creating a pucker of unguided regret, pulled at a couple of his ribs.

"Well," she said. "Probably plenty of people get married for less than sound reasons."

"Not everyone's as smart as we are," he said, and El laughed a little; and he did too. But it was mournful, because, he discovered, one of the beliefs he lived by was that his children were smarter than he was.

"Why didn't you want to tell me about the money?" he asked. "You said you suspected."

"Oh, Warren," she said. Her eyes were fixed on the windshield. "I guess I thought I'd say something if I was sure. You know." She turned the engine on; turned it off again.

He sipped her coffee, set it down in the cup holder. Turned toward the thought that was bothering him. Had he somehow caused this?

He hadn't minded giving his kids money, exactly, but he'd occasionally been. . . reluctant. Or often, really. They usually needed to ask for their allowance a couple of times, even when he had the right amount in his wallet. He'd been in the delivery office at the dairy, where the pay was okay but never lavish. Of course he'd wanted to give his daughter and son the agreed-on amounts; of course he'd been willing. But he'd felt a slight internal protest. That this should be a memory that came to him now, when he'd never thought of it before, and that it arrived fully laden with a boatload of guilt, seemed just and deserved. He caused this mess, or contributed, with his slowness to pay out ones and fives. Yes, along with his secret preference that the kids get a few more weeks' wear out of sneakers that were going at the toes, and his cheapness when it came to restaurants. But it was even more freighted, somehow; he hadn't felt that little nubbin of wasteful loss, had he, when he made, say, a car payment. And Lindsay had easily read all those undercurrents, he now felt certain. She was there at his elbow, noticing, and it was something important that an oblivious Warren never gave a moment's thought to, all through those years. Damage. Not just a bad few minutes, but permanent harm; and, moreover, harm that didn't appear until years later, negating any attempts he might have made to correct it at the time.

Now hang on, he told himself. You didn't necessarily wreck everything. She's an adult. There are plenty of factors and potential factors why things unroll one way and some other way.

Yet if he could just go back now, and gladly throw the allowance down on the coffee table. Hell, give them a raise, for no reason.

Well.

It would work out. Or not. Could turn out to be one of those intractable issues solved only once everyone involved had died, when it was finally all forgotten.

His sigh and Eleanor's overlapped, as they were so likely to do. What lay ahead now was swimming, the movie; he thought they should probably do both, to fill more time. And one of those brief conversational illusions came over him, as if he'd jumped ahead a bit and quickly jumped back again. He knew what was going to be talked about. How much he'd enjoyed walking that dog. Eerie-looking, though, greyhounds, with all those ribs. And of course the strange paleness of Swan, who looked like a tongue depressor. But there it was, his thought, and their narrow conversational path ahead, which he and Eleanor were reaching by, he knew, some practiced and silent consensus: that he was thinking he'd like to get a dog. That she thought so, too.

Tennis Lesson,
Orthodontist

I bought a plum-coloured canvas purse—sturdy; great size. On the front flap was a screenprinted zebra. Below the zebra's hooves, in a curly font, the mysterious words "I am more nervous than I look."

I loved that. Just straight-up tell the world! But, as with so much else in Japan, What the hell?

Why the hell?

I thought of my neighbourhood as the four blocks between my apartment building and the subway station—two straight lines, perhaps a kilometre. Logic suggests I might have explored that far in all directions, as if our building were the hub and I walked out a comfortable radius and back home again, but in fact I disliked the feelings of exposure and conspicuous foreignness brought on by wandering around alone. Mostly I went to work, on necessary errands, to raucous dinner parties at the homes of office friends, and to places my boyfriend, Takamasa, wanted to show me. Our outings were odd even when they sounded ordinary beforehand; just being on the other side of the globe, coupled with Japan's inherent weirdness, turned trips to the post office into adventures.

We got pricey tickets to a ceramics exhibition, where the famous pots turned out to be squat grey things I'd have overlooked at the thrift store. We ambled around the zoo (I had to turn away from the corner where one bereaved lion paced heartbrokenly). Taka found a tasting event for the year's Beaujolais Nouveau release; white-gloved, liveried men with stopwatches boomed out the instant the bottles could be uncorked, and we were all given condiment-size cups of wine, a portion I equated with a serving of ketchup at McDonald's. Japan was still rich then—it was before they went broke and began the long hard slog back toward solvency— and the country was busy hoovering up the world's top-drawer wine, coffee, Impressionist and Abstract Expressionist paintings, denim, and fresh figs.

I didn't fault them for this acquisitiveness: Even in my regular, non-wealthy neighbourhood, Japanese consumers operated with a level of scrutiny and appreciation, bordering on the scholarly, that I had never seen in daily life. At a café between my apartment and the station, every morning there was a new drip coffee; I'd purchase a cup of that day's Bolivian, Sumatran, Guatemalan, or Ethiopian and be told what to notice in terms of its aroma, balance, acidity, body, and aftertaste. Nearby was a shop, no larger than a bedroom, that sold only rare Beatles paraphernalia—hard-to-find vinyl, concert posters, buttons, everything archivally wrapped and exhaustively documented. I went in there once and, afraid to touch any of the costly relics that looked so unimpressive to me, fled in confusion.

Farther along that block was the rock store, where signs on the malachite walls indicated countries of origin, as if this were another wine outfit: South Africa, Namibia, Morocco, Mongolia, Peru. Unlike the Beatles place with its incomprehensibly high prices, the rock shop didn't intimidate me. I appreciated the sharp glittering crags of the stones, each placed lovingly in its own separate box, reminders that most of the universe was mineral rather than organic. And I gained a sense of how tough Japanese retailing was; every inch figured into the astronomical rents. I came from a country and a province that squandered space like oxygen, because we had more of it than we could ever use up.

I was reading a book that year on Toyota Motors and their just-in-time procurement system, and the shops in our neighbourhood brought those lessons home to me: Don't store your inventory yourself; have your suppliers keep it as long as possible. At the convenience store, everything was miniature—out of necessity, not for charm. Four-packs of eggs; half-size loaves of bread; little bottles of bleach. The place was like an anti-Costco. Running a business demanded a visceral understanding of the value of every cubit, every narrow countertop, and every item you chose to carry or drop.

Takamasa had given me the book explaining Toyota's management philosophy. It wasn't a work I'd have chosen, exactly—I was twenty-four—but he always hoped I could look on Japan with an adult and penetrating comprehension. He happened to share his given name with a famous architect, Yoshizaka Takamasa, who, among other things, had introduced Le Corbusier's work to Japan. (Le Corbusier! I'd needed a little refresher course; I'd heard of him, sort of.) Taka was curious about

Yoshizaka's buildings, and we planned to travel to Tokyo that summer to see his National Museum of Western Art, a deft blend of our backgrounds that felt like a benign prediction for our joined future.

Taka and I had met and fallen hard for each other during our third year of university, in Spain, and then he'd made three month-long trips to visit me in Manitoba. Yes, I'd try living in Japan with him, I thought, with the same eager curiosity for novelty a war bride might have felt. We set up housekeeping together in December and I turned a houseplant into a Christmas tree. Learning the neighbourhood and furnishing our new apartment was an extended, effortless joy. We browsed for the right bathmat, salad bowl, bedside lamp, all made with careful proportions and well-finished corners, all deeply pleasurable to touch. We lifted kettles to see which fit most comfortably in the hand. Everything we bought gleamed with meaning.

He set the alarm for me every night but woke up before it rang, because he liked to get up early. I'd wake to the sounds of him puttering around our apartment—unloading the dishrack; putting a load of towels in to wash—and over the months I came to know precisely what each little click meant. I could tell when he set the blue mugs on the shelf and when he was putting away the striped ones. And I could hear how quiet he was being, how careful not to wake me. When he sensed I was stirring, he'd come and get back under the blankets and reach for me.

We lived together nearly a year before it crashed. Taka didn't get out of bed for two days. Depression. He'd had it forever; it came and went but came back again.

Why was I just hearing this now?

Because he had thought it would never return; he had hoped, believed, the miraculous transition to a life constructed with me would make him safe for good. Why hadn't he warned me? Because I was the best thing ever to happen to him, so he had thought he was cured.

Couldn't he at least get up? Get out of bed and talk to me in a chair?

No. He could not get up.

Though after another anxious day and evening he did, of course, and he went back to work; but still everything shattered. I started to see what we were dealing with here. And now, treading my difficult path along the sidewalk each evening, there was silent clamoring and shouting inside my head. I faltered near the dark rock shop, at the locked café with its aroma of the world's great coffees seeping through the diamond-paned glass. Prepared myself to reach for my keys. I had to unlock our door and step inside. Forced myself, every evening. The fact that he'd been still alive the previous night didn't mean anything for tonight. And his being there at the end of a day brought no rest—only bedtime, then getting up and leaving, to come home again and see if he was alive.

I brought him pies, sweaters, blues CDs by querulous old men I couldn't understand and couldn't bear to hear—I'd buy anything I hoped might distract or please him—but the issue was larger than I could address. It was that, week after week, he longed to be done with living. My presence was no solace to him anymore; empty air.

One of the last times we talked, Taka posited that I was a magnet for depression. Neither of us understood how else we'd ended up together—his sadness was, until nearly the end, both dormant and invisible. I hadn't realized yet that melancholy woos its natural companions. A flicker of expression, an unnoticed thought, is easily detected by someone attuned to them. Others might miss those signs, but I was alert.

After I'd phoned his family and tried to explain, after we broke our lease and got our shining household goods divided up in ways that weren't too unbearable, when we had said goodbye, hugging and sobbing, and he apologized again and again and got into his taciturn brother's car and was driven away, I was left in a still-foreign country, now alone. I kept my teaching job and found a different, less honeymoon-like place to live and set about assembling the next stage of my twenties. I met another man, a fellow Canadian this time, and fell in love again, though it took a couple of years. He kept his apartment, and I had mine. Just before we left Japan together to commence a shared life back in Toronto, I placed the kettle Takamasa and I had bought four years earlier, which still looked perfectly good, on a lunchroom table at work. I wrote "For anyone who needs a kettle!" on a Post-it note, said goodbye to my colleagues and the office staff, and summoned the elevator to the ninth floor for the final time.

After my years in Japan I was pained to leave, but I had located an ease that was always rolled up inside me, and I was taking that back home. Like a souvenir, but both useful and enduring.

Kyle and I had been in Toronto a month when I went to Designer Fabric Outlet and, among the thousands of bolts of material, found a robin's-egg-blue linen for eight ninety-nine a metre, low enough that I didn't feel obligated to skimp. I made floor-length curtains on the sewing machine my parents had bought me in high school. Kyle hardly complained during the two weeks my fabric was spread across our living room. Nostalgic for Japanese standards of quality, I lined each panel with pale pink cotton. They turned out as well as any sewing project I'd ever tackled; I measured carefully, and the lining gave them a drape I was proud of.

"They're the nicest curtains I've ever seen," Kyle said. "The colour, the way they hang, the pink side, everything."

"You've just never looked at your curtains before," I said, but I couldn't help preening and secretly feeling like a genius, and I gave my sewing machine its own table in our tiny sunroom.

I had a one-year contract with the Toronto Transit Commission, gathering and sorting information on ridership issues, and Kyle had begun a master's program in public policy. Our apartment, one of four in a brick house built in the twenties, was in a residential neighbourhood near High Park, where, in the dying days of winter, we cross-country skied. Once I got ahead of myself and nearly flattened a toddler; after that I dialled back my willingness to follow Kyle's suggested routes and used my judgment.

In general, I felt he had too much innate conviction, and he believed I was overly conflicted. He thought I should keep less clutter in the bathroom and I thought he should eat fewer samples at the grocery store; but our arguments did not frighten me.

I took an ikebana class at the Japanese cultural centre, propping branches of forced plum or forsythia blossoms at precarious angles in affirmation of a belief that the late, cold Ontario spring would in fact arrive. We had people over and served stew and flan.

Some Friday nights we fell into a laziness like jet lag. We'd stay up until three, then spend the afternoons in bed, hands entwined, sleepily admiring the ways we were not alike.

We got a schefflera and, from the SPCA, a kitten we named Paulette. In April we borrowed a car and drove out to Don Mills to buy Ikea dishes—they started breaking right away; none lasted more than a couple of years—and a more successful dresser, which groans when you open the bottom drawer but which we still use.

That June we had a visitor for eight days. Kyle's friend Asher, newly divorced, was moving to B.C. and needed a place to stay first. I was intensely interested in him before his arrival; pity always expanded my heart. Staying with Kyle and me would, I imagined, be comforting. I mustered my tact concerning his wreckage versus the arrangement Kyle and I had, which was unfolding in ways that inspired cautious optimism.

Asher arrived with suitcases and two bottles of Gewürztraminer to drink on the splintery back deck that we had furnished with plastic chairs from the grocery. The three of us sat watching the resident raccoon family heave themselves into the maple near our back fence. The adolescent kits still followed their mother's path, skilled little hands stretching tentatively each time they reached for a higher branch, even though they acted fierce enough to navigate Toronto alone.

"Nice backyard," Asher said. "You could garden back here." He had barely glanced at me since he arrived, and I felt obligated to try to engage him.

"Do you garden?" I asked; it seemed to me like an old-folks' thing.

"Well, probably not anymore," he said, and poured more wine. Slumped in his chair, he looked closer to forty than thirty, and moth-eaten with despair.

Still, he had the energy for forceful opinions on many topics, from Korean barbecue to George Brown College to Switzerland's military service. "I need new running shoes," I told him. "What kinds do you think are good?"

That's the thing with letting men lecture: Usually we don't invite it, but sometimes we do, out of fatigue or simple kindness, or from the distilled Christian charity of *Well, bless his heart.*

I kept thinking Asher would warm toward me; instead he grew more pointed. All this *why*. It was disguised as interest but felt like badgering. "Why do you not use the clothesline?" (Um, smog?) "Why can't you bike to work?"

After a time I thought, *Well, two can*, et cetera, and asked, "Why do you think things started becoming difficult in your marriage?" It seemed like instructive information and I figured he would enjoy dispensing some wisdom, but I waited until Kyle was in the kitchen, not wanting to chance the disapproving glance I thought he might give me. True, I liked to be nosy; but in a well-intentioned and rescuing way that was usually welcomed.

Asher began, "It was just. . ." but didn't finish. His hand made a mid-air gesture, something that looked meaningful but that I couldn't interpret. He dragged off his glasses and rubbed his temples as if he might burst. I'd been too direct, and I regretted trying to give him an opening to confide.

"I'll make us some coffee," I said.

He did share, though. He told us that after his wife left, he started having auditory hallucinations.

"What are they?" Kyle asked.

Asher said, "It's like the echo of an explosion, without hearing the blast itself. Like waking up a second later."

"Ohh, I know what you mean," I said. "I used to get those a lot."

"Really?" Kyle asked me. "When was that?"

"High school," I said. "I had migraines, and these echo things. Not noise, but like its reverberation in my brain. Sometimes it woke me up, even. This feeling that there'd just been a loud bang, even though there hadn't. My parents took me to a bunch of doctors."

"High school! Man, that's a tough time all around," Asher said. Which could be true, I guess.

By Tuesday—I have always found Ben Franklin to be remarkably accurate about his houseguest advice—I realized how exhausting Asher was; he reminded me of high-school boys I'd half-hated and, unwillingly, half-liked. (Guys I'd gone out with once or twice, in some murky blend of attraction and antagonism. Guys who told me I had "a lot of potential." Meaning I wasn't there yet, but don't give up hope.) I was glad he was going, and in fact that weekend was the only time I ever saw him. And yet when the talk was simple, and Asher wasn't emanating an air of scornful challenge, I thought it might become a lasting friendship.

He told me things about Kyle I'd never have heard otherwise. One February when they were roommates Kyle came home in the middle of the night without a house key. Not wanting to ring the bell and wake Asher, he slept curled up in his jacket on the unheated second-floor landing, outside their apartment door.

"One of the most miserable nights of my life. I nearly froze," Kyle said.

"He was so polite," Asher said.

"You were so sweet!" I said, charmed even this many years later by his good manners. That automatic reluctance to impose.

The last days we filled with activities—museums; the boring Hockey Hall of Fame. We took the ferry to Centre Island and, looking back at the skyline, he said, "I'll remember how peaceful this week has been."

"I'm glad it's been good for you, man," Kyle said. "I'll be wishing you the best."

"I've felt like kind of a stray dog," he said. "The two of you, and then me."

I still had an itchy feeling that conversation with him remained mostly unspoken. That since he'd arrived I'd been beaming out clear signals, *Let us help* or even *I can help you*, and he'd been stubbornly refusing: *I don't want your damn help*. But maybe it was something different, more like *There's no help to be had*. I got the feeling he thought I was lucky to be with Kyle. And I did; I was. I just wanted other people, other men, to believe Kyle was the lucky one.

In high school, I had one task: keeping my father alive. When I got home each afternoon he'd be grading papers, with crackers and grape juice at his elbow. "Hi, sweetie," he'd say.

"Hi, Dad." Backpack. Shoes. Jacket. I never added, "You're still here."

Only late at night, when we were drinking tea in the den and my mom was sleeping, did he sometimes describe his unendurable sorrow. "I can't stand it. I can't take this anymore. I'm going to put myself in the ground."

"Dad, Dad." Scrabbling for the right phrases. I needed him. So did his students. Plus, Mom and I would never recover. Anything I could think of.

He said he couldn't go on. Nobody tried harder, but it was more than he could stand. He was, he repeated, going to put himself in the ground, that he had to do it; I always saw him being lowered into a rectangular, earthen-sided box of air.

"You're the best part of my life," he would tell me. Worn-out sentences. "You're the reason I'm still alive."

I was afraid to go to bed and leave him alone—afraid even to go make more tea when he asked me to. Especially if he asked me to. In between those sessions, he never mentioned dying, so I tried to extract promises while remaining vague. Even though he talked about it openly, I had to evade where I could. "Don't do anything today. You won't, will you?"

Like trying to hold a fish. I pleaded with my mom to help, but she had no better ideas than I had, and less patience. I skipped sleepovers. I phoned our doctor at his home, seeking advice. (Nothing.) When Dad drove me somewhere—tennis lesson, orthodontist—I begged him to come inside rather than wait in the car. I suspected a quick readiness to act that in fact I never glimpsed in him, a slyness that I figured he was concealing. I reasoned that he wouldn't take his life in front of anyone, so he couldn't be left alone.

I vowed to explain ten times a day how much I loved him and made tally marks on my notebook to keep track. If he went to the basement, I found reasons to follow. I baked cookies to thank him for remaining alive.

Asher was the last man I felt that distinct urge to boost up, to rescue. I settled into my life with Kyle. We got engaged; married. That's been twenty-four years.

I don't know which signals drew Takamasa to me, or what convinced me I could pull Asher up, possibly against his will, with my readiness to understand like a safe cape. Afterwards I thought his visit had been a warning—that my help would be no good to him, and that he wouldn't want it anyway. Moreover, I saw what a paucity of explanations we have, in western culture, for why one person in a couple might grow preoccupied with someone else. I disliked Asher more than I liked him, but still his presence was agitating and compelling to me. Many men, I've often thought, would have gotten furious over that, mistaking it for infatuation; Kyle did not. It gave me a sense that I was making a sound decision. Which turned out to be true.

My father died at seventy-seven, after a stroke. Until the end, he sometimes expressed a wish to be gone, though not with the conviction he'd had in those chaotic years of middle age.

My daughter Emily, who's sixteen, believes life has unfurled smoothly for me, that her childhood and adolescence have taxed her in ways that mine did not. She says this even though I've been frank with her about my past. And who knows; maybe she's right.

This summer she wanted new curtains for her room, and Kyle said perhaps I would make her some.

"Your mom sewed the nicest curtains for the first place we lived," he told her. "It seems like they were pink on the back side?"

"They were," I said, pleased he still remembered.

"That was a great apartment," he said.

Emily said, "You guys had such a great life. It sounds so fun."

"Yes," I said.

Emily fills so much of our daily routine that it's hard for me to believe how little overlap there is, really, between my lifespan and hers. Stacked against her life, mine seems to have begun in the ancient times. Hers will, I suppose, continue and continue, a long thread being pulled out straight. There's nothing between but the stories. Most of them are forgotten, and then we pick and choose among the rest.

Nosy White Woman

Clare's brother-in-law, Jonah, has come for the Canadian Thanksgiving long weekend, bringing his enviable single-person rituals with him. Before he turns in each night, he cleans both his phone screen and his glasses with a lint-free cloth, saturated from a pink spray bottle he keeps tucked in his jacket pocket. Also he microwaves the dish sponge daily during kitchen cleanup—a hygiene trick Clare has aspired to but has never had the wherewithal to get behind. And Jonah is accompanied on this visit by his dog, a crumb-coloured female Chihuahua named Davis Love the Third; he brushes her teeth several times a week, using beef-flavoured toothpaste and a rude fingertip brush with rubber bristles. He demonstrates, kneeling on the dining room floor as Clare and Kenneth hover with interest. The goblin-like dog rolls her eyes up at them, showing her cataracts, pleading for dignity.

"Upsidaisy," Jonah says, righting her and letting her go, the way kindergarten students release their newly emerged Painted Lady butterflies into the air—with a puff of genial confidence and an outstretched hand.

All Jonah's attentiveness to combating microbes, germy smears, and various types of build-up does seem to Clare somehow at odds with his appearance, which has a kind of earthiness his brother certainly doesn't lean toward. Jonah arrived at Clare and Kenneth's home in Ontario on a hoary morning wearing giant leather sandals that show his thick toenails. His feet look perfectly clean; it's just that Clare has lived with men with such toenails, and she remembers how it sounds like a heavy-duty stapler whenever they get the clippers out. Not dirty, but tough. Jonah isn't wearing cologne, but his striped pants look as if he would be heavily redolent of patchouli.

Well. This is just prejudice, of a sort. A stripe in pants fabric, which can seem to communicate so much, means nothing; or little. The same with bushy hair. Jonah is completing an HVAC diploma and works for a furniture upholsterer part-time, and they don't care if he's a woolly hippie.

She's inwardly relieved though that Kenneth, who's two years older and forty pounds heavier, nonetheless carries a lighter, more polished air. You can tell he shaves closer and has more grooming products in his arsenal.

Jonah also talks in an ironic throwback way that can leave Clare caught short in conversation. It's something she notices when they're getting pre-meal snacks ready. "I dig Vietnamese food," he says. *Dig*. At Kenneth's request, Jonah is searching through the cupboards, moving around forgotten vinegars and bottles of fish sauce with salt crusts around the rims, looking for something to pair with the cheese and crackers he brought. Clare, who thinks of herself as so polite, has had a couple of glasses of wine and accidentally says what she's thinking: "How long have you been talking like the Happy Hooker?"

Jonah asks, "How do you know how the Happy Hooker talked?" Then, perhaps because he's also had a couple of drinks, adds, "Let's ball, baby," in what is clearly a quotation but hangs in the air like a suggestion, making Clare blush deeply and bend to rummage long and thoroughly in the crisper drawer for some celery.

Jonah looks unable to believe those words have come out of his mouth. He makes his eyes wild as if in apology but adds nothing more, only silently lays crackers in tidy rows on a plate, staring at them intently. Kenneth, who never gets agitated about awkward moments, tells Clare, "Our parents used to have one of those books, up on a high closet shelf. Okay, who wants a beer? Or should we open this Chardonnay? The label calls it steely. They use steel barrels instead of oak."

"Steel barrels," Clare repeated, seconding the change of subject. They sounded like something for storing radioactive waste.

"You might not like it much," Kenneth told her, and explained to Jonah, "Clare loves all those Chardonnays with a ton of butter and toast in them."

Just the description made her mouth water. Though it also sounded like wine that would be favoured by the youngest drinkers, an alcoholic version of comfort food. What you would drink while getting over the flu.

"Think I'll hold off a while. I'll have some water," she told Kenneth, who was gesturing questioningly with the new wine bottle.

"Always a sound idea. Water all around," Jonah said, getting three glasses down from the cupboard.

"Later," Kenneth agreed, sticking the Chardonnay back in the fridge. He opens the oven door to take another poke at the browning turkey, which smells like meaty butter and the start of the holidays and coming home.

Clare and Kenneth have been married three years, and she's vaguely aware of how many patterns and habits of mind have fallen away in that time. It feels as if she's settled, the way the cereal companies describe in small print on the side of a box. For instance, she's lost the internal need for bilateral symmetry: if one of her legs bumps against the edge of the sofa, she no longer has to tap the other leg to correct the unbalanced feeling. That had been a lifelong thing, until, quite recently, it simply disappeared. Similarly, velvet doesn't bother her anymore, and she's even beginning to like it; well into adulthood, touching it gave her a smothery, clotted feeling in the back of her throat.

So some of her interactions with the world are simpler. Clare attributes this evolving not to her marriage but to the maturing of her brain's various lobes and segments. It feels like something to celebrate: Fully Adult. And other things, social things, are easier now. Thanksgiving this year is small and no-stress, just family; in past years, even with only two guests, she would have had longer lists and a little shoving sense of anxiety that would have been always greedy to expand itself.

Besides Jonah, the other guest is Clare's mother, Brenda, who's driving the sides across town around two. She's bringing mashed potatoes, a fancy squash thing, coleslaw. Kenneth has made brownies from a boxed mix, and that's dessert done; finished. They're having their dinner today instead of on the Monday because Brenda will be heading down to Florida that day. She spends the winter there, in the house where Clare grew up.

Brenda's relationship with Kenneth has by now progressed from polite liking to a mutual joshing; she has not met Jonah before. He was living in China when Clare and Kenneth got married, and after he returned to Canada he lived in British Columbia.

The three of them are watching videos in the tiny office when Brenda arrives with her quick "beep beep" of the car horn and all the bustle of coming in laden. She has special carriers just for transporting serving dishes.

"I'll just pop these in the oven to stay warm, if that's okay," she says, unloading. "Is there room for them in here? Goodness! You've been busy!"

They haven't been that busy but appreciate the reflexive compliment. Clare gives her mom a squeeze. Brenda sorts another bag and produces a bottle of inexpensive California sparkling wine, and everyone else agrees they've sobered up sufficiently to open it now.

Brenda likes both Jonah and his dog, and she understands immediately, in a way Clare hadn't quite, why Jonah had settled on the dog's name. Some golfer.

Brenda says, "It's the verb followed by an adjective that makes it such a peculiar name. Love the Third. Like Davis Bring My Blue, or something." She looks at Jonah with approval, for having brought a grammar-related element into the gathering.

"Exactly," Jonah says. "I always used to think he had the oddest name I'd ever heard. Like, love what, exactly?"

"Davis Love Your Fellow Man," says Brenda, scratching Davis on top of her little walnut head. "Love the Third Person in the Family."

Brenda seems to enjoy Jonah in the same way she always likes being with Kenneth, and Clare has a sense of abundant, jolly ease dispersing through the snug kitchen. Breadsticks, olives, the brie and crackers. Persimmons sliced on a plate. No one eats those, but they look nice. Clare and Kenneth recently bought some comfortable chairs, which make a big difference. Brenda hardly ever drinks, maybe one glass at someone's wedding and on a holiday like this, but Clare has noticed that her mom has a gift for capitalizing on the truth-serum effects of other people's alcohol consumption. It's not done from a troublemaker's stance; rather, she's a friendly opportunist. Within an hour she has uncovered that Jonah feels lost in his Estimating Job Costs class, that he might buy a used pickup, that he and his girl-friend may be coming to a natural end. Stuff Clare and Kenneth might have learned over six months, if that.

Then Brenda somehow winkles another girlfriend story out of Jonah, one Kenneth and Clare never heard when it happened. He says, apropos of something Clare has missed, "And my ex-girlfriend smashed the window in my front door last year."

Kenneth says, "Really? Sarah did that? You never told me that."

"Yeah, it was pretty bad," Jonah says. "She left, and maybe ten minutes later she came back and smashed the window with a softball. Then she left for good, and I haven't seen her again."

Kenneth asks, "How do you know it was a softball?"

"She left it on my porch. I ran to the door and saw her marching down the front walk, giving me the finger."

Brenda says unexpectedly, "You know, something similar happened to me, many years ago. One of my ex-boyfriends took a baseball bat to my car."

"Mom! Are you serious? When was that?" Clare feels transiently apologetic toward Jonah, switching the conversational attention from his assault so quickly; but how has she never heard this before?

"It was, let's see, maybe two years before I met your father. I had a little Datsun. You know, they became Nissan later, which was strange. And I left work one evening—I was working at a health clinic in Moore Point, and I was the last to leave that day—and there was all this shattered glass on the pavement around my car. I remember it looked like diamonds."

"Good god," Kenneth says.

"It was scary," she says, looking around the table. All three of the younger people are sitting back in their chairs, watching her. Davis is folded on Jonah's lap, her ears swivelling around in receptive listening mode, ready to catch a word she cares about—"treat" or "out." Brenda says, "I felt lucky that I never saw him again. He didn't do anything else."

"But that sense of danger," Clare says. She is moved by the idea that her father appeared sometime after this, repairing, fixing. Even if the patch didn't last forever.

Kenneth is fidgeting with a couple of persimmon seeds, which are like smooth brown wooden marbles. He says, "What sounds so scary to me is that he must have waited until your coworkers had gone."

"That's right," Jonah says. "You were really vul-
nerable."

Clare asks her, "What did you do?"

"Swept the glass off with a file folder and drove
home," Brenda says.

That night in the living room, when they've had brownies and pie and coffee and played two games of Sequence,
Clare asks her mom about her preparations for the trip
south and the winter away. Brenda, who is sixty-eight,
has not so far displayed any addle-headedness or signs of
incipient dementia, no real night-vision trouble or dire
forgetfulness. Still, it's a long time to be so far apart.

Kenneth asks, "Do you get nervous at all about the
drive?"

"Not really," Brenda says. "I've been doing it over
twenty years, and this will be my fifth time going down
alone. Since I got divorced," she explains for Jonah. "I
stay with cousins and friends on my way down, so that's
nice."

"Yeah, you're not likely to run into any trouble,"
Clare says.

"No, I never have any real difficulties," Brenda says.
"Get bored sometimes, but I stop if I get sleepy. It's
highways all the way, and of course I have my phone."
This leads to a lengthy discussion of phone plans and
add-on travel minutes.

Clare is reminded of something she has not thought
about in a long time: her family's practice of calling the
police if they spotted something questionable. When did
she stop? She'd learned it from her parents, who both
did it. They called the police if a small child seemed to
have gotten lost, or if someone looked high enough to

be at risk of wandering into an intersection. If help was needed.

They generally used the local, non-emergency number, rather than 911, to demonstrate an appropriate but not hysterical level of concern. It felt like participatory democracy, like being an upright citizen. Doing their duty to the community. Clare had taken for granted that everyone did this, or at least that they ought to. And that soon some police officer, someone like the alert fellow who holds up traffic so the baby ducklings can safely cross in the picture book, would just swing by and check things out, maybe shine a flashlight around and call in an all-clear on a police radio with a curly, old-fashioned cord. That was her notion of how things unfolded after she hung up.

Did she think it was based on fact? Well, it had been her reality, obviously. Nothing but respect and helpfulness. She had been startled to discover that in other families, most families, people didn't do this.

She says, "Mom, you don't ever call the police anymore, do you? I mean, you realize you probably shouldn't?"

Brenda says, "Shouldn't what anymore?"

"Call the police. It's different now," Clare says.

"Different, why?"

"You know; we know more. Police brutality and all."

"I'm not afraid of the police, Clare," Brenda says. "They don't worry me one little bit."

"Oh, for god's sake. I didn't think you were. I don't mean brutality toward you."

"Toward what, then?"

"Toward Tamir Rice. Philando Castile. You know this stuff. Eric Garner, Mom. Alton Sterling."

"You're talking about black people who were killed? By the police?"

"*Yes.* And often it seems to start from these really small things. Tiny; nothing at all. And the situation can escalate so quickly. It's just not something to get involved with. Horrible stuff can happen that you have no control over."

"Those things aren't typical, though. That's why they're news stories—because they're unusual."

Clare says, "I'm not sure that's exactly true."

"Really? Do you really think those tragedies happen all that often?"

"Well, I don't know; they sure seem to," Clare says. "Please don't bring the police into people's lives anymore."

Brenda asks Kenneth and Jonah, who are not eager to jump in, "Are you hearing all this? What's your take on this?"

She is frowning at Jonah. He raises a hand slightly and shakes his head. Brenda's accusatory gaze jumps over to Kenneth, who rolls a seed under his palm and says slowly, "I have to think Clare's probably right about what can happen. And that it's beyond your control, and maybe it's better not to call unless it's really clearly an emergency."

"Well, you never used to hear about all this police brutality," Brenda says. "It's kind of a new thing, it seems like."

"Mom, no. What's new is that everybody has a cell phone now that records video. And things can be posted online by people who witness them."

"Well," her mother says, voice turning stringy with disapproval. "I don't know about that."

About what, the posting online? Recording the police? Brutality and unwarranted shootings? It was more a general pushing away than anything specific, Clare thought. As if Brenda were saying, "No, no, no," but not in answer to a certain question.

Perhaps Brenda feels exposed and wants to guard herself because Kenneth and Jonah are hearing all this. Kenneth, with his outsider-in-the-family status; and Jonah, whom Brenda's never met before. And Clare does feel for her mom; she does. Kindness itself. But surely that's not what matters here? She has a small guilty awakening remorse that this conversation is one she neglected to tackle before now; she hadn't realized she had a duty as a younger, in-the-know person. How could she not have thought of it during previous years?

Involved, she'd said to her mother. That police brutality incidents aren't "something to get involved in." When what she meant is that they aren't something to start.

"Mom, promise me," Clare says.

"Promise you what?"

"That you will not call the police to report a person who is black. Or otherwise of colour."

"Clare, really. Of colour. Really."

"We probably shouldn't even report white people. But promise me you won't report anyone of colour, for anything, ever, even if you happen to see something that seems clear-cut."

"You know I am not racist. At all."

"Nobody's talking about your being racist! Or not racist! Or anything at all! This is not talking about you. I'm just saying, as for me, Mom, in my own case, I used to think it was helpful and, and, *correct*, the right thing to do, calling in problems. Or possible problems. I thought it was my civic duty. And now I no longer think that, or not in the same way, and I would never do it now."

Brenda says, "Even if you saw something. That you thought should be checked out. Not trying to get anyone at all in trouble, just looking in on something."

"That's right. I would not."

"Even if you saw a hold-up."

"Even then," Clare says, knowing perfectly well that she's lying to make her point—she would dial 911 if she saw a hold-up. Also, she thinks, who says hold-up? Where did her mother get this Dick Tracy vocabulary?

Brenda says, "I suppose I'm just a nosy white woman."

Kenneth puts in, "Brenda, kindness isn't being nosy. No one is faulting you." But even that "no one is" sounds like ganging up: three against one. Brenda looks the slightest bit placated, though.

And Jonah says, "It sounds to me like it's not a matter of blame. It's more like. . . making use of new information that's come to light."

"That's exactly right," Clare says. It's a solid phrase that she mentally grabs onto—dispassionate and official-sounding. New information that's come to light, and which can't be argued with.

Her mom says, "I think my judgment is perfectly sound, Clare." She lifts her mug and takes a slightly shaky mouthful of tea. "I feel as if you're blaming me for something I haven't done."

"No, of course I'm not doing that," Clare says, possibly unhelpfully.

Brenda says, "As if I would ever do anything to lead to anyone's death."

"You're not the problem if someone dies in police custody," Kenneth says.

Clare is thinking about the story of her mom's vandalized car. The shining broken glass; the drive home, not knowing whether he might be lurking, or following, or waiting for her back at her apartment. And how much it must have meant, taking for granted that police officers were always going to protect her.

Now she can tell they're getting near the end of any remotely useful conversational trajectory, and she is trying to make every word count. She says, "It's just that, in trying to do the best possible thing, there is the possibility of contributing to a bad outcome. Which could have been avoided."

"I will give that some thought," Brenda says, and they leave it at that. There's a slight shift in the conversational air that indicates it's finished. Kenneth gets up for more tea, and Jonah takes Davis outside to empty her tiny bladder once more before bed.

Clare is touched by both guys' thoughtful diplomacy with her mother. Their patient silence, and then their stepping in with verbal pats and reassurances of concern. She can see that both her husband and, she thinks, his brother, whom she can't read nearly as well, are stopping themselves from urging Brenda further to lay off the helpful calls. Of course Brenda doesn't want to be racist; that's obvious. And, perhaps more pressingly this evening, in the lamp-lit living room with her homeowner son-in-law and his artistic brother, she doesn't want to be thought racist.

Or maybe that's not fair. The lopsidedness is what's still bothering Clare, though—all this care given to not hurting Brenda's feelings. As if her feelings were the ones that mattered.

After Thanksgiving, the month marches along. Halloween is still going strong in the stores, but Christmas has begun to appear; Brenda has been in touch from Florida several times, and all is fine down there. No snags or difficulties, and she's been swimming twice a day and plans to send Clare and Kenneth a carton of citrus fruit.

Clare has been trying to sort through an impression that's been niggling at her since she and her mother argued at Thanksgiving. She's thinking that parents never quit their children; never. But adult children do turn from their parents. That's what it means, all this "Thy people shall be my people" business.

Over the past year or two, it feels to Clare as if she's been lifted and set back down a little differently; a realignment of her axis seems has taken place. She has transitioned from a family-of-origin orientation to a generational one. Her primary loyalty now is to Kenneth; after him, she feels a trusting inclination toward the perspective of people around her age. They're who she tends to believe.

She realizes, with a tiny shock, that she will replace her mother. Brenda is fading, and Clare will slide into her slot. She will put on a scarf and step out into the brisk air and be counted.

Christmas Cranes

One bright fall afternoon I was on Pinterest browsing pictures of window boxes, while also trying to figure out why anyone would want to be Speaker of the House.

I fixed on a set of copper ones, the kind of thing I'd never seen in a residential application. Maybe as part of some commercial, exceedingly fancy outfit, like a Breitling or Hermès storefront from a magazine ad in an American neurosurgeon's waiting room.

But they were, first, not typical for Atlantic Canada, and would perhaps cause unwelcome attention or envy among our neighbours, offsetting the benefits of their looking so great. And, second, even if they weren't all that valuable, everyone knows about copper theft; perhaps I'd be setting us up to have these lovely things yanked loose from our house with crowbars, then sold in some junkshop for six dollars. Get home from the grocery store and see denuded brackets dangling there.

So I wasn't giving my full attention to the House Speaker developments, because Paul Ryan was still saying no, not running; sorry, guys; and no one else was really coming forward either. Steve Scalise—of the "David Duke without the baggage" reputation, back when we still innocently thought that made him unacceptable—was apparently not going to step up; Darrell Issa was making rumbling noises; Jason Chaffetz wasn't getting any traction. I was waiting to learn whether Boehner was going to be condemned to stay on as Speaker, thus bringing to fruition the nightmares he claimed he'd been having.

The Hill reported that Louie Gohmert had accused Boehner in a closed-door meeting of acting like a dictator by delaying the vote. It wasn't clear who Gohmert thought would have prevailed. It reminded me of watching the 2009 RNC chair election play out, when Michael Steele finally defeated Katon Dawson by 14 votes in the sixth round of voting. I remember Steele bounding on stage to make his speech, and how, back then, I thought we were seeing some strange moments in politics.

Except, of course, that Steele and Dawson both wanted that job. Now nobody wanted to be Speaker.

You have to figure Boehner's a much happier man these days. Plus, Scalise ended up getting *shot*, for god's sake. Though fortunately he had health insurance and could recover.

My husband, Simon, returned home and I clicked my Pinterest tabs shut, because I knew what he would think of my window box aspirations: too fancy; out of our league; how would we mount the things; plus, who the hell polishes their window boxes? (Sound point. I wouldn't want to do it myself; yet I wouldn't want to see him up on the ladder, with its little heels half-heartedly grabbing the soft soil at two different depths.) He had just come in from voting. Election day, with its vic-

tory for young Trudeau junior, was still ten days off, but
Simon had picked up his mom and dropped by the poll-
ing station so they could get it out of the way.

The straightforwardness of this made me jealous.
Alabamians would weep.

"What's up?" he said, all breezy and satisfied over
his errand-running success and his country's impecca-
bly straightforward democratic processes.

Well, why not, I thought, and turned my laptop
toward him. "You know we were talking about window
boxes for the front of the house," I said. "I was looking
at some online."

"Oh, yeah? Good. We could spruce up a little."

I began cautiously trying my luck, the way you do:
"Take a look at these. . . ."

He was all, *Whoa*, is that *copper*: expensive; fancy;
polish; bracket; etc. Watering. Ladders.

He'd thought I meant modest white plastic, the
kind he had in mind.

This gap, man. This gap.

Our son Austin's project for his school art fair this year
involved painting miniscule scenes onto his discarded
contact lenses and displaying them on a lightbox, so
the watery landscapes were cast, magnified, onto short
vertical panels. The piece was called "Things I've Seen
and Things I Haven't Seen." His execution was sloppy
but truly charming—as he switched on the lightbox,
suddenly those small bulges, like water drops placed on
the diffuse white surface, threw radiant amateur vistas
against the little walls he'd tilted up in place.

When he got to the chaotic gym and was setting
up, though, he learned of a clause he hadn't noticed in

the guidelines: No body fluid art was permitted. There was back and forth over whether contacts he had worn included bodily fluids. Clearly the administration had reasons for wanting to avert any high school "Piss Christ"-type controversy. (Austin's project happened to involve neither piss nor religious imagery of any sort, tending instead toward teeny, not-very-skilled indications of a dog on a hill, a brook in a meadow, and the like. Foliage and scraggy branches he could do with the tip of a pointed paintbrush.)

The principal's decision: The lightbox was okay, but Austin couldn't use the contact lenses to project the painted scenes. So he set up his glowing cube and his blank white panels, the size of paperbacks, then stood there for an hour, gamely answering questions from parents working their way around the gym. And when prizes were announced at the end of the week, he won honourable mention.

Austin is in grade eleven and starting to look at universities, and suddenly this kid, who'd never shown an interest in art and was taking the class for an easy elective, was musing about applying to art schools. It was as if walking up to the podium to collect a ribbon had transformed an empty accolade into something meaningful.

Simon and I agreed, privately, that he was delusional. Our dismay was tempered with amusement and resignation; only Austin's immaturity allowed him to feel proud of this imaginary achievement. His lack of interest in producing a portfolio seemed likely to solve the problem for us. At the same time, what a pleasure, that this crazy kid could keep surprising us, keep being so young.

His friend William, who's a year older, has been touring universities, and Austin got the idea of going along to visit NSCAD, the Nova Scotia College of Art and Design. Thirty, forty years ago, it was all about conceptual art, and that still reverberates in this part of the country, at least in memory. Given the wholly conceptual nature of Austin's near "win," this didn't seem like a bad fit, but Simon and I couldn't seriously imagine his enrolling there. Even now, talking about applying, he continued to show no interest in art. We dutifully signed him up for the open house anyway.

Austin came home from touring NSCAD with a nylon messenger bag, a meatloaf-patterned phone case, and an expensive-looking second-hand copy of a book by an artist I'd never heard of, Jenny Holzer. The title was "Abuse of Power Comes as No Surprise."

"Maybe he'll go into political science," I told Simon.

Later that week, Austin said the school wasn't for him. "Doing art seems like a really cool, fun thing, and I could picture myself there, but somehow—you know. I'd have no clue how to come up with hip ideas all the time. When I was working on my lightbox project, I thought it would be great if I won, but probably I'd have lost interest before long."

"Good to know," I said. "You don't even need to think about it yet."

Secretly I hope he'll end up doing something green, something helpful. Solar. Wind. Be the change.

One of the lasting comforts of my marriage has been the near-psychic moments. It's less as if Simon and I are reading each other's mind than a sense that we're listening to the same station. A song heard on the radio in the morning can weave and twist through the day, joining us both in an invisible count—hours later, one of us will murmur, "The Sultans played Creole," just as the other person is silently thinking it.

I used to think this made us special and intended for each other. Over the years I realized it made us normal people who are able to count beats. Still, it was one of the low-key reassurances of everyday life; they stitch us together and help fend off divorce. If I'm slogging through a week with a lot of moments when I kind of hate Simon, it can help that we have the same soundtrack running in the background.

Recently, however, my inner soundtrack has gotten more in synch with Austin's, less with Simon's. It made sense that Simon and I were both swivelling toward Austin, whose years in our household were nearing their end. How momentous and strange, that he would be moving out: Of course we were attuned to him.

Because Simon, too, seemed to be chiming in with Austin's tuneless bursts more often than with mine. Standing in the kitchen one morning, I heard Simon upstairs rumbling, "When you put me on the Wolverine up to Annandale," while Austin, down in the laundry room and too far away to hear him, was singing the same line.

It was similar in the car. Typically Simon and I noticed things at the same time—not always, but frequently enough. "Is that sign new?" or "Look at that white branch." We were mostly prompted by a fall of light across a certain plane, I'd concluded years ago. Now, though, it was as if Simon and I were looking in different directions. Suddenly it was with my son that I tended to spot things at the same moment; and he and his dad also seemed to share a common eyesight. For this final couple of years, I thought, Simon and I both wanted to be standing where Austin was standing, seeing what he was seeing.

I heard voices in the driveway at the same time as Truck, the aging Airedale we inherited from a neighbour who went into a nursing home. His eyes opened and found mine, he on the cushy Big Hug pillow that babies his joints; me on the sofa—gazing at each other but listening to the outside. I hoped my sensory attunement wasn't going to shift now to line up with the dog's. Truck, though frail, was intelligent and charming enough to be married to, but it discouraged me to think I might be losing ground among my closest relationships so steadily.

The noise was Simon and Austin unloading a propeller they'd bought at a thrift store, something Austin wanted for his bedroom. "Watch your fingers!" Simon called. They were trying not to let it touch the snow; the thing was wood, much longer than the bed of the pickup.

"Nice purchase," I said, holding the door back.

"Thirty dollars," Austin said. "I'm wondering if I could hang it from the ceiling. Feel how smooth this finish is, Mom, where it's not dinged up." I felt the propeller, which seemed pleasantly but not unusually smooth.

Sometimes a first time jumps out at you; that was what I realized while I admired Austin's haul. Had he ever before shown any interest in decorating his room? He'd never expressed a preference for a duvet cover, a rug, a calendar. "Sure, that's fine," was all he ever said; his bedroom was a jumble of unrelated furnishings that migrated there from other rooms and, once set randomly in place, never seemed to move again.

His propeller must have pleased him—over the next weeks he took to lugging in barn boards, a scale, a barrel stave, a didgeridoo, a handful of wrenches; and he began arranging vignettes of the busted and the broken-down not just in his own room but in the kitchen, den, and bathrooms. I told Simon that Austin reminded me of an Upper Paleolithic youth working out the earliest principles of embellishment and decorative arts. Apparently his day as a young artist among his peers had made an impression.

However, this new tendency to rescue, hoard, and display was the only lasting effect we saw from Austin's art school excursion. He didn't mention NSCAD again, and he went back to musing about biology programs and whether Quebec would be too cold for him.

Being the only one in our household who follows U.S. politics isn't ideal, and yet there's something bracing about being in this alone. I still vote in South Carolina, by absentee ballot. Simon knows little about South Carolina politics (except the name of longtime Democratic strategist Dick Harpootlian, which he likes to sing out at random moments and once used when we played Charades). I prefer it this way—I don't want to get into my current take on Nikki Haley or my inconstant feelings about Lindsey Graham, who keeps losing the grudging respect I'd granted him but then winning it back again. Explaining it all to someone else would be too much, so staying current is a private indulgence.

Except that I don't want to anymore.

It's such a change from the previous decade. I can hardly bear to read now, after years of obsessively following what was happening. All the time he was growing up, Austin kept urging me to focus instead on Canadian politics—he felt slighted by my lesser engagement with the country we actually live in—but there's not enough daily action to attain critical mass and hold my attention. I don't care as much about news stories as I do about the turning of the inner gears, and in Canada it's hard to get a good clear view of that.

And here's the beauty of the Christmas tree industry, which is our business: There can be a lot of downtime. We hardly sleep from October through the end of the year, and in summer we're up at dawn, grading and pruning. But there have been stretches when I was able to hole up in the office and devote myself full time to reading about politics—twelve-hour days, for weeks on end.

Maybe I've kind of been cheating on Simon with Barack all this time. He got an inordinate share of my attention; and now that's over. I can't believe how gone from my life he is.

I know three women my age who are planning to file for divorce as soon as their kids finish high school—a neighbour, a college classmate I'm in touch with, and Simon's cousin Lori. They all claim to have actual plans to bolt the minute they figure they've done their duty. The marriage that made me think I'd be wise to lean into my own, though, isn't one of those; it's my sister Patty's. She doesn't seem set on leaving her husband—she has simply made their lives as separate as possible.

She's long had her own toothpaste, which is maybe a bit unusual but I didn't think was odd; after all, people have their own toothbrushes. But, as the conservatives like to warn, a slippery slope is hard to get off. Every time I'm at their house, there's more evidence of separateness. Differences not just of type, I've thought, but also—unfairly, shamefully—of quality. His-and-her salad dressings and ice creams and laundry detergents and stacks of washcloths; and, always, one seems better. Two kinds of coffee beans waiting to be ground; separate little dishes to hold keys on the hall sideboard. They are like East and West Berlin.

She has her own salt.

"Well, Nate doesn't like what I like," she told me, when I suggested it was odd and getting odder. If she has to pick up his clothes from the floor, she uses a wooden spoon, as if lifting a garter snake. It's not a marriage you'd want to be in, given a choice. I wonder if Nate might also be putting together a plan to get the hell out of there. I love Patty, and I always will. But any reasonable person has a limit. She is here in my life as a warning, I tell myself sometimes.

"You've got fewer than a hundred weekends left before you'll be starting university," I told Austin one day as he was deftly parallel parking in a short space.

"I know," he said. "I've counted." He and I were picking up the window boxes Simon and I had ordered—made by a local guy; simple wooden rectangles, painted a pale blue. I wanted to plant nasturtiums.

It was February, with a bleak sky but disturbingly warm. The walls of snow that had been pushed to the edges of all the parking lots were melting, and the tires made a pillowy, voluptuous "Sshh, sshh," noise as we drove.

I was caught in that state you reach of trying to hold in your mind appropriate regard for past, present, and future human and animal misery while not succumbing to the urge to take your life and get it over with.

You know the experiences I mean. The sight of a bird (bee; butterfly) makes you want to kill yourself, because, as recently as one generation ago, the sky (yard; vacant lot) was filled with them; so where the hell will we be in another fifty (thousand; ten thousand) years?

Well. I've been pushing back despair enough long years to have figured out what mostly works for me, most of the time. Take action where you can, but otherwise try not to think about it. Advocate for sound policy. Keep the focus either immediate or extremely long term—thinking about the middle years, I'm afraid, will kill me.

Turn your mind away; it's not made to withstand what we're living through. We are cursed to be the people having to witness this diminution, this transition. And my job is to pass along to my son the resilience to endure the watching, to keep focused on it with an appropriate level of rage and grief; and yet also cultivate and hang onto the means to be profoundly happy.

Simon and I were in the office settling invoices. Truck came in, laboriously heaved up onto the loveseat, and released the deep sigh we call off-gassing.

"You know what I love about Truck?" Simon pulled off his glasses and rubbed his face. We've both reached the age of constantly putting on and taking off our glasses.

"His energy and vivaciousness?" I said.

"The way he stares at me sometimes. You know how dogs and cats peer right at you, so steadily."

"Sure," I said.

"I was thinking, when it becomes longer than another person would meet your eyes, when with a person it would become uncomfortable—I really like that moment."

My thoughts rose up in silent protest; Simon and I used to spend long, long moments gazing at each other. He doesn't need Truck for that. Yet how many years has it been? This good person whom I've lived with for so long, I thought. Not loneliness, but nonetheless something sharp. A loss.

Austin's latest art class project involves photography.

"Christmas what?" I asked Simon.

"Cranes. Construction cranes. You know, at job sites they decorate them with strings of lights."

"Oh, sure. Sometimes they decorate a tree in the cab of the vehicle."

"Yeah, or in a bucket, up in midair. Here, you can see his photos." Simon had just picked them up at Costco for Austin.

"Well, that sounds promising," I said. "Original." I'd always enjoyed those decorations in a mild way; now I found that simply giving them this moment's attentive thought was increasing my appreciation, and I was startled at how appealing, how charming, they seemed. I pictured someone inching along the horizontal length of a crane, laying down strings of lights. No; impossible. There was some other way, which I couldn't imagine.

And the trees! The whimsy of them, looking so elfin, flanked by diggers and graders. Why had we never partnered with these folks? I paged through the shots, trying not to leave fingerprints. Austin's photos weren't tightly composed; all were at night, and a few were blurry. I loved them, though. Like nearly everything about Christmas, they were both cheerful and melancholy: the barren, moon-world sites; the long constellations of dim light strands. The trees like brave jokes. One glowed from the cab of a small mover, which dangled from the raised front quarters of a much bigger vehicle. Every photo pulled at me.

"When did he take these?" I asked Simon.

"We drove around a couple of evenings," he said. "He had a few subjects. Grocery stores were one. Water towers. He liked these best, though, and I think he's right."

"They're lovely," I said. "Imagine thinking of this." I wondered if they really were special, or if I just wanted to think my son had something.

"I know," he said. "Good eye."

Sometimes I think Austin is like a distillation of me and Simon—the two of us, reduced by half. We wanted to have more children after him but couldn't make it happen. God knows I'm not thinking about grandchildren, but I can see why people ache for them. What a relief it must be, to see that bottleneck widening out again, to know, *Okay, there's one more generation I'm good for.*

Not that we can take credit for him. Certainly at his age I wanted to be *sui generis*, and I imagine he does.

It's not my own despair I most fear, I finally understood. It's Austin's—and not now, but long after I'm gone, when he'll still have so much to watch and endure. Not merely all the things we know will be hard because we've lived through them, but all the new, additional burdens he'll have to withstand as well. My sorrow and guilt and worry extend so far into his future. I was still picturing the construction worker, the one I'd decided doesn't really exist, crawling patiently along the crane to lay down those bright strands. But he can do it, I thought that day, gazing down into those photos with their delicate tracings of light. He will gather the strength; from Christ knows where, he will find it. He will be okay.

My

Gary Lehtinen was touched by another person for the last time at the grocery store, four days before he died. He bought pretzels, blue cheese, canned pineapple, and Sprite, and he paid with bills. When the cashier, Gretchen, handed him his change, the side of her hand rested on his palm for the second the quarters and dime fell, though this contact didn't register with either of them. Then Gary carried his reusable black bag out to his Subaru. Last time carrying that bag; last time home from the grocery store. Final moments thrumming past the car windows like an invisible wildfire.

Back in the store, Gretchen closed out her register and headed upstairs to the staff break room, where her co-workers Jillian and Edson were watching anime videos on Edson's phone and finishing subs from the deli counter.

"Hey, Gretch. Want part of a sandwich?"

"No, thanks."

"It's the chicken one you like."

"Nah, I'm good; thanks." A tangle of lettuce was heaped in the plastic container at Jillian's elbow, and Gretchen knew without asking that she was taking it home for her son's rabbit, Baby. There were things Gretchen liked about her job.

The narrow plastic loveseat that was her preferred spot was unoccupied and she lay down with her feet on a milk crate. She had grown skilled at break-napping here. Gretchen let her eyes half-close and drew in her awareness like a snail's horns. The previous day she had lost the button from the waistband of her pants, and now a stiff corner of the fabric jutted out; from where she was lying, it looked like a small triangular erection just below her waist, visible even with her apron on. She patted it down but it sprang up again. Gretchen was smart but had not learned to sew on a button, so it would not get fixed; eventually it would draw comment in the break room, forcing her to buy a new pair of black pants—money that, on her cashier's salary, she resented spending for something so dumb. She would think of buying sewing supplies and trying to fix it without really knowing how, but in the end buying seemed simpler.

Now Edson and Jillian scooped up their napkins and sorted their garbage. It was a matter of debate among the staff, how much the sorting mattered. Even in the staff room, though, most people did it.

"See you, Gretch," they said, and she murmured, "Bye," and fell closer toward sleep almost before the door swung shut behind them. It was rare to be alone in the staff room, and peaceful.

Gretchen would never notice that Gary Lehtinen didn't come in anymore. She had seen him a couple of times a week for the five years she'd worked at the store, but only the most attentive would miss even a regular among a crowd of other regulars, and Gary was one of hundreds. A couple of the store's employees would see his obituary, but they didn't comment on it among themselves—customers' obituaries were, obviously, a frequent occurrence—and Gary's absence was never mentioned by anyone at the grocery. No one knew that Gretchen was the last person he touched. Apart from her family, there was no one else of whom that would ever be true, but it was an unnoticed connection, unknown even to the two of them.

Tuesday afternoon Gary was outside for the last time. Ross, Gary's neighbour on the left, saw him and waved.

"My daughter and my granddaughter," Ross called across the driveway, signalling toward the woman and girl who were standing by their car. Gary knew about this daughter—Ross had only recently learned of her existence, and here she was, living just five hours away, grown and with a child. Overnight: a grandfather. Gary and Ross sometimes had a beer on one back porch or the other when the mosquitoes weren't bad, so Gary knew how much Ross wanted to become part of their lives.

Now Gary waved back and ambled over, feeling shy, and was introduced to this clearly nervous woman, who lifted her daughter up onto her hip and busied herself with the child's birdlike needs.

"Aren't you a cutie," Gary told the girl. She wore sandals, a diaper, and a pink t-shirt that said Littlest Feminist, and she clutched a stuffed toy seal pup by the tail. It brought memories back to him of how children hauled their toys around by the most convenient appendage or grip, often the neck.

"This is Chloe," her mother said in that drawn-out, translating tone mothers use, and Chloe put her arms around her mom and buried her face.

She was wearing bear ears, Gary saw. "Were you a bear on Halloween?"

The girl shook her head and tilted her face a bit to tell him, "A werewolf."

The three adults laughed. Chloe watched them watching her to alleviate their adult awkwardness. Four white people, two of them uncertain but glad, one benignant, one fretful and worn out, passing a moment in the heat by a car with an open door.

"You're a plum, all right," Gary told Chloe, feeling that he was repeating himself. "My."

"Look at those lashes," Ross said; and it was true— Chloe somehow had longer eyelashes than any of the grownups.

Gary said nice to meet you, enjoy the visit, goodbye, and he crunched back across his pea gravel driveway. It was the last time he was to take those two pleasurably grinding strides that had been his main reason for choosing pea gravel; but he didn't notice those footfalls this time.

Back on his own side, Ross watched Gary for a moment: He had the genesis of the thought that Gary was looking older this summer; then Michelle, who was finding her nervousness impossible to contain even though this was now the fourth time she'd seen her newfound father, asked if Ross wanted to walk somewhere to get lunch. They could take the stroller if it wasn't too far. The weight of the shyness Michelle and Ross felt when extending such invitations to each other, if it could have been measured, was more than Gary had experienced in the past twenty or thirty years. So Ross looked back at his brand-new daughter and granddaughter, didn't finish his thought about his neighbour, and no one saw Gary step up onto his porch and through his front door for the last time. He closed the door behind himself. He had now breathed his last outdoor air, seen people for the last time. He was finished speaking, aside from a couple of idle remarks and exclamations to himself.

Had Gary known, walking along his front porch railing and up the three steps, that he was oblivious of the final opportunity he would give himself to take in the yellow and white rosebuds on the bushes his wife had planted, he might have thought losing that moment was a tragic shame. Or he might have thought it didn't matter.

Which were both true.

Gary was last mentioned while still alive by two women sorting donations for the upcoming Lutheran church book sale and flea market. Pam and Coral were working in the church hall with four other volunteers on the afternoon before Gary's death, getting things ready for Saturday morning. The sequins of overlap between Gary's life and other people's were becoming so few.

"I think Gary Lehtinen's older daughter brought these boxes in," Coral said. "Did you see her?"

"No, I haven't seen her in a few years now," Pam said. "He usually sends some nice books and things." Gary had rarely felt up for church the previous couple of years, but he found the offloading of unneeded possessions to the flea market nearly as satisfying.

"Here's a nice picture," Coral said, using both hands to hold it for Pam to see. It was "The Flower Carrier,"

with the worker weighed down by his gargantuan basket of market flowers.

"Oh, that's—who is that? Diego Riviera. We used to
have that in my elementary school."

"This?"

"Well, a print like that. It's famous."

"Is it?" Coral said. "What for?"

"He was a socialist," Pam said. "It's about the
exploitation of workers. Did Gary and Sue have it up in
their house?"

"Must have," Coral said. "Do you think five dollars?"

"Yeah, maybe. The frame's nice. Wood. Say seven."

"It'll never go for that."

Pam said, "You're right. Five."

The picture had hung in the Lehtinens' breakfast
nook since before the children were born, and they grew
up looking at the flower seller trying to manage the
weight of his massive pink burden. His fingers, splayed
flat on the ground to help him rise, reminded each Lehtinen child at some point of bananas, a connection that
took them several years to discover and was invariably
mentioned when they were back at their parents' house
again for holidays.

Fond as all three children had always been of the
Flower Seller, when they were grown and gone none
of them felt an urge to take the picture and display it
in their own homes. Gary sat at the breakfast table side
with his back to it, rather than facing it, so weeks could
go by without his noticing it.

Coral and Pam and the rest of the team sorted until
six-thirty, then knocked off for the evening feeling good
about the sale's fundraising potential. With practiced
eyes they swept their gazes over the tables assembled in

the church hall. Maybe four thousand, forty-three hundred dollars; something like that, they thought.

Gary had less than twenty-four hours still to live but had not yet begun to die. Yet, for so long, connections to him had been trending this way: fewer, shorter, dimmer.

Gary was last seen thirty-five minutes before he put a hand to his chest with a grinding feeling. In the shower, a minuscule spider, speck-sized, gathering itself in the corner behind the soap for the week, watched Gary come in for his morning routine. A daily occurrence. It waved some legs at him, threat behaviour, when Gary's vast hand descended for the soap, but that alarm passed without incident. Gary left the bathroom and dressed, rested, did not feel right. If he had had someone with him, he might have said, "I wonder if I'm going to need to get you to take me to the hospital," speaking in his idiosyncratic way that packed unexamined nuances of doubt, obligation, and persuasion into his exchanges. Gary sat on the bed, stood up; sat on the chair, stood up. Lay down on the bed. Worse, but somehow easier to lie down. Since the tiny spider had watched Gary walk out of the bathroom and disappear from view, he had not been noticed or watched by any living thing, and he ceased to notice anything outside himself. There was a lubricated, slipping quality to the moments, with a sense of looking through the hole in a spool. Everything he could still see turned silver.

Gary Lehtinen's final candle went out on April 27, when Peggy DeGraw died. She had known him when she was a child. Gary's relationship with her father had been an oddly small-town and old-fashioned kind: Her father had once employed Gary, and Gary had, for a time, employed her father.

Peggy was ninety-one last April. Afterwards there were people still alive who had seen or spoken to Gary, but she was the last to have known his name and have hers known in return; to have exchanged conversation with him; and to have had some kind of crisp impression of him as person rather than a passerby. By the time Peggy died, she had not thought of Gary Lehtinen in more than fifteen years. She had no idea, of course, what particular fragile scrap of memory she was holding within an abandoned fold of her brain, and she would not have been able to care much, beyond a wispy, untethered puff of interest, even if someone had told her she was the last on the planet who had known him. Peggy's memory was shot by then.

The unreachable recollection she possessed was of how Gary talked to animals and insects, reprimanding and sometimes swearing at them with an idle specificity. "Holy crap, toad!" she heard him say cheerfully when a brown arc, tracing an elliptical perfection as if launching itself over a half-buried egg, curved up from the grass and vanished again. "You made me jump!" Peggy was nine then, and it was the funniest thing she'd heard during her long, boring month of drooping around the backyard while her father and Gary—Mr. Lehtinen— were building the two-bay cinder-block garage, where her father was expanding his auto repair business. Gary said, "Shoo, squirrel! Get on outta here." He even talked to creatures Peggy had never heard anyone address directly (and never would again). "Let's go, worm; move that pink hinder." He spoke as if he were using capitals, as if these were the proper names of individual creatures called Worm, or Bug, and distinct from every other one of their species.

Decades later Peggy would think of Gary Lehtinen briefly at a Toronto Blue Jays game, when she heard announcer Buck Martinez urge, "Go on—get outta here, ball!" A pocket door in her mind slid back to reveal a forgotten closet, and there waited Mr. Lehtinen; he'd been present all along, unneeded and unacknowledged. Or not him, after all, but a good flat picture of him, a fine likeness, some page from a magazine or chapbook in the attic—a thing you flip through in a perfunctory way simply because it's so old (before tossing it out, also because it's so old). The short filmic memory of Mr. Lehtinen prodding that worm with his square-toed brogue, being so careful not to injure it, also came back to Peggy, bringing a little additional richness. For a few seconds he was dim but astonishingly present, alongside the rough, hand-hurting cinderblocks; the pile of sand where she made toad apartments, molding damp sand around her bare foot and then carefully withdrawing it; her father's thin nylon dress socks, in colours, with wingtips; the sycamore with its peeling bark her father forbade her to pull loose; and the family's relative prosperity in those years when her father repaired cars after work and on the weekends. Then a woman three rows behind her caught a foul ball; Gary Lehtinen and the garage and the toads vanished from Peggy's thoughts like a flame pinched between a damp thumb and finger, and she never thought of him again.

The memory remained in there—losing potential each year Peggy aged, but still real, still one living bead among millions, like a headful of caviar. Accessible, a way to reclaim the past, rather than to usher in the future. All of us are both-ways Janus, constantly choosing where to point that gaze.

There were many more times that she thought of her father. Slipknots of connection kept working free, though, and, as one of those, Gary drifted away from her family and was as gone as if she'd never seen him.

Binoculars

Kendra's mother came by one night close to bedtime to put a toy sloth on the heap, and I went out to see if she'd like some cheese and crackers. She'd told me that what she had for dinner most nights was a can of frosting eaten in front of the television. No cooking, and no dishes to worry about.

She and I were in a tide-like relationship—she added toys to the collection, I silently took them away—and we seemed to have found a stasis or point of agreement on an appropriate size for the pile. When Kendra first died, things got really out of hand, with the slogan-bearing teddies arranged in tableaus and artificial flowers strewn around. Mylar balloons bobbed on their ribbon leashes. Look, this is my *yard*, I finally said, but Neva had created or found an artistic outlet and was not going to be deterred. She said, It's the edge of your yard; it's not like they're right in front of your house. And she promised to keep it under control from then on.

This apparent concession was hard for me to refute. I own the whole stretch, and it's true that the crash happened not right in front of my home but a little way over. I got home just afterwards—I actually heard the tires screaming as I was nearing that last curve—and no one was on scene yet. I stopped my car at the end of my driveway, then realized emergency vehicles might need to park there and got back in and pulled forward, quaking so hard I ended up sore for a couple of days; parked near my usual spot, then got back out and ran to the sedan. It was upside down, and Kendra was on this side. Whether because she was nearer, or because she was a girl and so I identified with her, or because I was already kind of blaming Dylan for killing her, she was the one I tried to talk to, though I've never been able to remember what I said. Then I ran around to the other side to check on Dylan. Of course I didn't know their names yet. Then I ran up to the house to call 911, though I had to turn around and get my purse from my car and find my house key. I didn't think of using my cell phone, for some reason, and I dumped my bag out on the back porch to find my key, and the way it all tumbled out and bounced and scattered around made me fall down on my knees. Things rolled through the gaps and disappeared (my back porch floor is slatted—a design flaw, I have realized; and, though I can get under there through a hatch-like door, I've never known what those things were and never wanted them back). I couldn't stand up and had to crawl fast over to the door and use both hands to get the key in the lock. There were still no other cars: everything seemed to be on me. Got inside, phoned, and ran back down. Dylan had died while I was up there calling, I think, so I stayed at Kendra's window and held her hand. She was twenty-two; I didn't know that either.

No seatbelts, was what one said. A paramedic. That was why. He was talking to his partner, not to me; there must be a code of ethics that prevents them from commenting to bystanders. I had been too overwhelmed to make sense of what I was seeing. I remember hearing his quiet answer, because then it struck me that I was inside a Driver's Ed video, like those they showed us in high school. As if after all these years the warning had come true. Which I guess it had, though not for me.

For weeks afterwards I'd be falling asleep and hear the extended, complicated crash—you know how they have a beginning, a middle, and an end—and I'd jolt awake, the way you do, and try again to keep Kendra alive a little longer. We stared and stared at each other— there seemed to be nothing but her eyes and my eyes, and a sort of hollow glass tube between them, it felt like, something with weight and solidity that was attaching my gaze to hers. I've wondered if it felt like that to her, like we were staring at each other through clear binoculars; she looked real to me, but maybe I looked very small to her. Maybe I was shrinking.

Her eyes were brown and her gaze held on and held on, with a question I had never seen before. I wonder how different it might have been if someone else had been in that seat, dying; I suppose there are as many ways that could play out as there are accidents. I don't know whether the intensity came from her, or me (I don't think it was from me), or somehow me plus her, the two of us creating this dynamic that swept aside so much, because it happened to be her there dying and me there to help her do it. I was drafted as an acolyte.

I think the silent conversation we had was this: *Am I dying?*

I don't know.
Then, *Am I dying?*
I don't know.
And again, *Am I dying?*
I think so.
Then—it seemed inevitable, though it wasn't—*Am I dying?*
Yes.
Stay here.
I will.
I tried to breathe for her, but of course I could not.

It was ten days after the accident that Neva came to see me. I had gone to the visitation but not to the funerals, and at the visitation I signed the book but was spared having to speak to the families, who were besieged with well-wishers. It was like the whole town in one room; I must have seen forty people I knew. So when Neva dropped by my house, not calling first, I was unprepared in the moment but had been, in some larger sense, expecting to see her sometime soon.

She had driven to my house a roundabout way, though all it spared her was passing the immediate scene of the crash. It was about thirty feet beyond my driveway, and of course the skid marks gave an explicit and vivid account.

Friends and relatives had been putting teddy bears and flowers down, and I'd thought I'd gather them up at some point and take a few of the more attractive ones to Neva and Don. Everything had gotten soggy—the teddies were mostly those dollar-store ones filled with pellets, and now they were heavy-bottomed in a way that reminded me of a toddler with a saggy diaper.

Some of their colour had already leached out, even in that short a time in the sun and weather, and they all had grimy high-water marks halfway up their bodies. I couldn't imagine Kendra's family would appreciate these grit-covered, molding things. I tried a few in my washing machine, but they tended to fall apart; it was a mess.

So I thought Neva had come to take some of these away. She did take a few, but she rearranged the ones that were left. And something in the rearranging process must have spoken to her, must have helped snap Kendra's memory back into focus. A couple of days later I glanced out the window and there was Neva, puttering around, and this became her creative memorial outlet.

Now she was talking about buying that patch of land from me and turning it into a park. A "parkette," we said, agreeing that it was a funny word, one of those you can't believe is real and actually appears on legitimate signs erected by some municipal department. The humour and general goodwill between us, and my liking for her, covered the alarm I felt when she first broached the topic. Not only did I have no plans to sell a chunk of my land, I had less than zero interest in having an ongoing, evolving memorial to Kendra a few yards down from my driveway culvert. That was the crux of it: Neva saw this as a permanent arrangement, like a headstone or a named building at a university, while I saw it as a temporary accommodation I was making during the time her grief was the sharpest.

I'm not a believer, and I gather Neva and Don aren't, either. But this loss knocked her sideways, and the spot where Kendra died was the place she kept being drawn back to. More than the cemetery where her ashes are buried. Maybe Neva felt instinctively that, if she had been there holding Kendra's hand rather than me, she would have done a better job of anchoring her with the living. And maybe that's true.

I have been on my own for twelve years (I was widowed young, at forty-five), and seldom do I miss Arnaud more than when I have a sticky problem with someone outside the family. He had excellent common sense along with an equally useful gift for managing boundaries and conflict. I have often tried to shoot myself back into our past, or tried to bring him back to life to give me advice.

And so—what? That question occupied me during the hottest part of July. I thought about Arnaud being there, in the realm of the dead, with Kendra. (Not that I believed that sort of thing.) How would he advise me to help Neva reach her again?

An answer came to me over a few days, gaining clarity until I felt certain. Kendra needed rehoming. Neva and I, together, would have to contain her spirit and move it.

My son, Miles, likes to send me books on creative thinking—Edward de Bono and whatnot. You might ask yourself, say, How would a fork approach this problem? Or, What would a bat do? And he bought me a creative-thinking card deck by Brian Eno and somebody, which I nearly sent to the thrift store during a purge but hung onto out of sentiment. Now I get them out and shuffle them around from time to time, mostly just to justify not having gotten rid of them and also with the idea of pleasing Miles. I'm old enough that a gift still feels like a bargain to me, and using one seems like living up to my end. (Miles isn't that way at all: he'd say, "Mom, if you don't like something I give you, for god's sake don't hang onto it"—and then be disappointed and deny it.)

So I fished my Eno thinking cards out of the sideboard and turned one over. "Use an old idea," it suggested. This was not illuminating. Next I drew "Decorate, decorate"—the opposite of what I wanted. The following card, though, read, "Tidy up," which was more the direction I wanted to move in. Then I got one that said, wistfully, "Ghost echoes."

I sat looking out my dining room window at the goldenrod that masses in the field across the road, the curse of late summer in Nova Scotia, when I have to take Benadryl every day. I took that card and my little friend "Tidy up" over to the kitchen and stuck them up on my fridge and stood there studying the words, how they were just shapes. Little slashes and curves inked onto paper. Back at the table, "The most important thing is the thing most easily forgotten" seemed to be turning up the still-low volume on some message. I had a feeling of trying to winkle something stubborn out of a cranny.

"You don't have to be ashamed of using your own ideas" was like Arnaud talking to me; I heard that one said in his voice. I set it aside to stick up with my others. One more, one more, I thought. "Go slowly all the way round the outside."

It came to me in the shower, the way ideas do. We needed to walk her there. I remembered hearing a great-aunt claim that a person's spirit could only travel as fast as a horse could walk. I was maybe eight or nine, but it made sense to me intuitively—the see-through human spirit; the plodding, patient horse; the cars racing by, too fast to keep up with. Kendra had loved biking. Neva and I could push her bicycle to the cemetery.

What was the ghost of Kendra that I wanted to help Neva move? I don't believe in spirits or an afterlife, and I don't think Neva had, either, before this happened. My gentle conversational realignments had not been picked up on with enthusiasm. Impossible for me to know whether Neva pictured a sentient eddy, or a low note linking the twigs and the insects and birds that moved past my driveway, or a white-sheet ghost like Casper, or her daughter as she was while still alive, but now translucent. A voice in Neva's head that she could converse with, and that grew stronger when she worked at that patch of grass? Or did she not think in those terms, but nonetheless find comfort and a sense of usefulness in shifting and moving stuffed animals so that the group's contours were pleasing and animals seemed to gaze at one another, with none of them left friendless at the edge of the pile?

For Kendra's trip I wanted a bicycle basket, the old-fashioned kind. Willow, as I learned from Martha Stewart's website. I drove to an upscale bike shop in Halifax for one. It was elegantly woven, the top edge a shallow curve that felt pleasing in my hand.

We decided we'd take the walk on Saturday evening, a quiet time, not much traffic between my house and the village. We would need to walk on the shoulder and hope we didn't get hit, but it's wide enough. Neva asked me what I was thinking of asking her: Would we look strange, two middle-aged women pushing a bicycle along the road? Nah, we concluded. We just felt funny because it was going to be hard.

Saturday morning I went to the florist and bought carnations, all colours, two dozen of them. Some I was able to thread down through the weave of the basket, to make a crown of blooms around the top. I trimmed the remaining stems and heaped the flowers inside. Flower arranging is not something I've done much of, but perhaps it's not that tricky, because it looked so complete when I finished.

Neva unloaded Kendra's bike from the back of her SUV and I brought the basket out to her. Even after all our emotional chats since the crash, it was now that I felt shy, handing this over.

"This is for you, for today," I told her, and then wondered if she would think I was only lending it to her and wanted it back. But her lips trembled—I saw she'd understood me in spite of my awkward phrasing, and we occupied ourselves with figuring out how to fasten the basket on, which you'd think would be simple but wasn't. It turned out we needed a strap that I'd left inside; I went back in for it, and we fastened the basket securely to the front and took our places.

"Which side do you want?" I asked.

"I think the right. Is that okay?"

"Sure," I said, moving over.

She said, "I used to carry her on my left hip when she was a baby. So it still seems kind of familiar, when I think about holding her."

"Sure," I said again, and the two of us started down my gravel driveway, pushing the bike along, holding the handlebars, with the idea of Kendra like a column of air riding on the seat between us.

We stopped at the cluttered memorial pile, and she chose seven or eight small stuffed animals to nestle into the basket, among the carnations' sturdy stems. The toys were so dew-soaked that I thought about a hybrid memorial trinket someone could market, with cut flowers pushed down into teddy bears as if they were floral foam. "Decorate, decorate," I thought; I'd been pondering those cards on my refrigerator since I put them up there. "Ghost images," I said to myself.

We walked on either side of the bike, not talking much, and my sense that we were in fact ferrying Kendra along kept increasing. It was as if she were with us. The wheels crunched along the gravel shoulder, a little chewing, grinding noise that both preceded and followed us, slowly, with the late August sun on our bare shoulders and the asters nodding gently on the roadside as we went by. The goldenrod was motionless in the lazy heat, and there was that early melancholy that shows up in Nova Scotia from mid-month on: a few leaves beginning already to turn, saying what no one was ready to hear. It was always the same trees, I'd noticed over the years, and seemingly even the same branches on the same trees that turned first. The sentinels.

We passed Dixon Harvie's pastures, and the place that sells blue and green eggs from exotic chickens, and the gas station and post office and credit union. We went over the little footbridge and stopped to look down into the rocky streambed, making its quiet chuckling sound. Neva stooped to pick up a pebble and let it fall in, and I wondered what she could be wishing for.

We were nearing the cemetery but were going slower and slower, like that Zeno's paradox that says you never reach a finish line if you keep shortening your steps enough. It wasn't evident who was slowing us down, me or Neva; the bicycle felt like the planchette on a Ouija board, moving forward of its own volition, but reluctantly. Neither of us—none of us, I thought—wanted to get there.

At the gravel lane past the United Church we turned right, and then we were at the old stone gateposts, and it was time to go through them. We stopped. The cemetery was small, maybe seventy graves, and the soft grass was like a calm green pond. On the obelisk-shaped post beside me were patches of green; I scraped at one with my thumbnail.

"Moss," I said quietly.

"No, that's lichen," Neva said, hushed. The cemetery was well tended, though, and a number of the graves had bright new arrangements adorning their sheetcake-like stones. I saw a teddy or two around and gathered that different rules applied here from those that governed the decoration of the roadside. Neva would be able to place things here but would have less scope for spreading out.

We wheeled the bike carefully down the centre path. I had no idea what Neva was thinking. I was saying silent goodbyes to Kendra, as many as I could fit in, as if she were actually perched there in between us and knew she was about to be set down and left behind. I imagined Neva's heart ripping apart like a sheet of stamps.

I helped her undo the basket—I hadn't known if she would want to leave it there, take it home with her, or throw it out, but she unbuckled it and lifted it off and became busy with the flowers and toys. "Kendra Michelle Rafuse," the headstone read, with her dates and a carving I'd never seen on a grave before, a V-shaped line of geese, flying off to one side.

"She loved to see the geese flying away and then returning," Neva said, running her palm across the engraving.

"It's pretty," I said, and it was. It had an elegant minimalism that the business at my yard hadn't led me to expect, and I was ashamed of myself.

"Neva," I said. I crouched down in front of her and held her shoulders. "I want to do what you want me to. Whatever you need now, that's what I want to do. Shall I stay here with you? Or do you want to be alone? Whatever you want is fine."

Neva took in the scene around us, and her gaze was baffled and exhausted again. "Oh, I hardly know," she said. She smoothed Kendra's geese again, and we sat there, with the bike lowered to the ground beside us and the willow basket on the grave. "I don't know what I want," she repeated.

I waited, and finally she said, "I guess I'd rather stay here alone for a while."

"Okay," I said. "If you're sure."

She nodded. Our legs were wet from the grass. The sumac trees at the back of the cemetery held up their red berry clusters. The daycare down the road was quiet. A pair of crows landed on the path, their wings gleaming like chunks of coal snapped in two.

"Do you want me to come back for you in my car, in a while?" I asked her.

"I'll ride the bicycle," she decided. "I think I'll just ride it on home, if I can leave my car at your place for a bit. Don and I can come over and pick it up this evening. Would that be all right?"

"That's fine," I said. "I won't be home this evening, but you come by and get it whenever."

"Thank you," she said. "Thank you for doing this."

"Neva, I'm happy to," I said. "You're so brave. I have so much admiration for you." Our hands caught and held, and then I kissed her on the cheek and turned and walked back along the path and started home.

A few weeks later I went up to the linen closet where I keep the rest of Arnaud's ashes. I lifted down the box and gently touched the grey gravel with my fingertip. It was still so heavy. I took out one small piece and drove over to the cemetery, holding it on my tongue, and got out and made my way to where the memory of Kendra now lay. I peered down at the grass, looking for a blade with a particular grooved shape; when I found a good one, I tucked the little pellet into it and gently pressed it into the earth. "Take care of her," I instructed Arnaud. I knelt and kissed the grass, and drummed my hands against it for a moment, then went home to call Miles and see what he'd been up to lately.

Clean

After Stokes gently tugged off the condom, balled it inside a tissue, put it down on the floor by the bed to toss later, and said how great that had been, he added, "I know it's still a long time away, but it'll be nice when we can stop using condoms." Liz, now nestled in the crook of his arm, didn't answer, though in her imagination her eyes shot open and she went, *Whoa; hang on, now*. She had no plans to stop using condoms, and it was news to her that Stokes had such an idea.

Still, they didn't intend to try for a baby for quite a while. No rush.

Liz and Stokes were living in Brockville ("near the Dollarama"); she worked in the intake department of the hospital and was thinking of studying nursing. Stokes worked at a farm museum, letting school groups help with shearing, or teaching interested people to handle a scythe—he'd established an annual scythe-mowing contest that was turning into one of the museum's most popular summer events.

Their small postwar house was sunny and quiet. One morning the cat, alert even in her sound sleep, heard a car in the driveway and popped her head up from her basket. "Someone here?" Liz asked her, and went to the kitchen door and looked out. "It's Mom," she said, and Stokes jumped up and made a quick sweep through the rooms, gathering up evidence of slovenliness, indulgence, or questionable taste, sweeping his hand over flat surfaces to dust them as he went by.

Liz stood on the tiny front porch to greet her mother, who wasn't supposed to be there and whom she'd be seeing on the weekend anyway. "Is something up with Dad?"

"No, he's all right this morning," her mother said, stepping inside and working her sandals off. "He should have a few more days of feeling pretty good now. He was sleeping when I left, but he has that new Henning Mankell book you brought him, and that yogurt he likes. I told him I'd be back before lunchtime."

"Is his mouth any better?"

"A little bit. That mouthwash helps with the sores."

"That's good. Come on in. You want some coffee?"

Stokes came into the kitchen, having hidden the gathered pile in their bedroom. "Hi, Rena," he said. "How's Calvin feeling this morning?"

"Oh, it's so hard on him. It just decimates him. It's very tough to watch."

Liz said, "Mom, you said he was all right today."

"I meant he's feeling better than he was last week. He's not doing better than he was a year ago."

Stokes put an arm around Rena and gave her a side hug. "Nearly halfway through, right?"

"Almost halfway," she agreed. "If we make it. Here, Liz; did I bring my tote bag in?"

"Let me check the car."

"Friends have been bringing us food and so on, and your dad wanted to send you some of the peanut butter cookies. He could only eat one."

Liz had gone to Calvin's chemotherapy training with him and Rena, before the treatment started, to learn what to expect and how to take care of him. It was alarming but sober, and set the tone for the dogged family culture they would need over the next few months. There was a plan for the mental part, the physical, for the logistics of hospital visits. Parking. Costs. Here was how to deal with middle-of-the-night medical emergencies. Head-down coping. Here was how to manage side effects. Here was how to deal with the toxicity.

They were given housekeeping regimens for handling bodily fluids after chemo treatments. His laundry had to be done separately; vomit would need to be cleaned up with great care; the toilet, after he used it, should be flushed an extra time, with the lid down; family members, remember not to touch pills with your bare hands. Calvin's body would be metabolizing what was pumped into him. Rena was in charge of all the systems. Liz was the helper.

Liz drove them back to their house in Peterborough afterwards. Her mom gazed out the car window, holding a Kleenex, while her dad rested on the back seat with his eyes closed. He wasn't feeling sick or weak yet, but the narrative of what lay ahead seemed to have punctured him internally, so the energy and courage he would need were already leaking out of him. "It's not the cancer that makes you feel so awful; it's the treatment," they'd been told by a couple in waiting room, when they struck up a cautious, genial conversation.

That sentence kept running through Liz's head now, and she wondered whether it was the same thought her dad was having. How strange for the cure to be the worst part.

Two deer picked their way along the ditch by the road. Liz slowed down to give them time to panic and bolt. They stared at the vehicle and passengers for a long moment. Then the panic seemed to come out of nowhere, like a wave that scooped them up, anticipated by the humans but not by the deer themselves. They managed to flee away from the car rather than into it. Liz wondered whether this was new to them every few days, as if they'd never experienced it before.

"Close," Rena said.

"Do you think they saw us, sitting inside here?" Liz asked.

"I'm not sure how good their eyesight is," her father said from the backseat, laying his head back again. "I saw an eagle in a tree last year, and I pulled over, and we stared at each other for a good long time. I remember thinking, it can see my face a lot more clearly than I can see it. It could have been looking at the backs of my retinas, the way it was searching me."

One thing she had always appreciated about her dad, Liz thought, was that he clearly had an interior life that he enjoyed, didn't mind sharing, and yet kept mostly private. He seemed to her to be a person who liked his own company.

"What kind of expression did you think it had?" Liz asked him.

Her father considered. "Assessing," he said.

After her father had been gone for more than a year, Liz and her mom planned a trip to Calgary, just the two of them. Her mom apparently had "always wanted to see the Stampede," though certainly Liz couldn't remember her ever mentioning this before. It was not the kind of spectacle Liz was interested in, though her experience with such prejudgments was that the event always turned out to be far better staged and more worthwhile than she anticipated.

Her trip came just before a pivot. Liz had turned thirty-two that spring and Stokes turned thirty, and they decided to start trying to get pregnant. In the fall, they said. A small gap; a couple of months to finish painting the basement, in case she got pregnant right away. It had been four years since the morning Stokes had mentioned that someday they would throw out the condoms.

Liz had always been a person who was careful about germs, a cautious person, with the conversations about handwashing and potential cutting-board contamination in the kitchen and the proper temperature meat should reach. All of that. But in recent years she had also heard so many mentions of various forms of disease transmission, of MRSA on hospital countertops and paper towel dispensers, staph bacteria on doctors' stethoscopes, the many elements contributing to a separate area of concern. Don't ever listen to the damn CBC, she kept thinking. Or pick up an Oprah magazine.

Moreover, there was HPV, the human papilloma virus, spread through contact and linked to cervical cancer. Even, lately, found on doctors' exam tables; *what the fuck*. And the women from Stokes's past—what were their stories?

And chlamydia, so easily transmitted, so often asymptomatic until you wound up infertile. Liz could still hear her health teacher preaching, "No matter what, even if you're on the Pill, you want to always use a condom to protect those delicate, delicate fallopian tubes."

And she had become so used to condoms. How clean they were. How separate and conclusive.

She left Stokes behind and flew with her mother to Calgary for four days.

As they were bumping their wheeled carry-ons behind them in the airport, Liz studied her mother to see how she was holding up. By the expansive windows of the terminal, the new slackness of Rena's skin showed so clearly.

"We could get a coffee here, if you want, before we go to the hotel," Rena said. Liz often had trouble figuring out whether her mom's innocuous statements held a message. She had never become skilled at it, but now she seemed to hear a tremor or something wistful, like the curled, shy tendril of a vine, trying to reach.

"Sure," she answered. "Let's find a coffee place."

They found a Starbucks and sat at the tiny table, so close to each other. "How are you holding up?" Liz asked. She took a cautious sip of her foam. Her mother's lower eyelids reddened, even before tears appeared, as if the crying began with her skin rather than her tear ducts.

"You know what I was thinking, flying here," Rena said. "Looking down at all those towns, neighbourhoods, houses. That every family is like a machine. It's like some intricate device, some kind of fiddly tool with gauges and gears that you'd see in the Lee Valley catalogue."

"A family's like that?"

"Yes. All these moving parts that make up the motor, and the motor is the family. And it's encased in its house."

Liz saw the rows of Monopoly houses again, from high above. Indistinguishable from one another, yet distinct.

Her mom went on. "And the job of that engine, that family, is to protect itself and keep humming along. He took care of me, and I took care of him. I think it's the only way things can function. All this work, this caretaking, goes on invisibly inside the walls of these houses."

"It's not public? Is that what you mean?" Liz asked. "It's concealed?"

"Well, not that it's hidden; but unexposed, uncounted. All this practical daily work, this caretaking, caregiving. It's like, I don't know, you can tell how many dogs live in Canada, because you can find out how much dog food is sold. But in the days when people fed their dogs table scraps, there was no way to count them. Does that make sense? All this family work—it's not being measured, but it's vast."

"Yes," Liz said.

"And if people had to pay, it would be unaffordable. Imagine trying to quantify it, trying to hire hospitals and aides to handle caring for the whole country."

"Oh, I see what you mean. It's a form of savings. An efficiency."

"Right. And I thought—Well, that's what a family *is*. Not only that, obviously. I loved him so much. But partly, yes, the simple fact of having a person to depend on. And it's important. We're these self-contained little units that handle our own business, clean up after one another, deal with the vomit even when it's literally toxic waste, flush the toilet twice because a drop of the urine is poisonous, keep going, do for your family, and so the larger society is able to get far more done."

"Mom, you're so philosophical," Liz said.

"Well. You know me," Rena said. She fell silent and sipped her black coffee. The reddened eyelids reappeared.

"What is it?" Liz asked.

"Now there's just me. No other half of my machine. I'm like a wrecked helicopter in a shed."

Liz covered her mother's hand with her own. Rena said, "There's the problem with the tidy system. One person is left over, after the end."

It made Liz think of the apprehension she had felt before her own wedding, when she tried to focus on the gravity of marriage. It was meant to last so long— decades longer than any project, relationship, contract, or loyalty she had ever entered into before. Daunting, but also heartening.

And, of course, there was that future waiting, a downed and busted helicopter.

Long before she ever met Stokes and had to think about what decades of marriage might involve, Liz had once found herself standing in a bookstore reading about fisting, which she had never heard of or imagined. Putting your hand, wrist, possibly forearm inside someone. She read with fascination that it was uniquely intimate, requiring new levels of trust and caution. Her clearest takeaway from the book, though, was that once you got your hand far enough up there to reach the neighbourhood of the distal colon, it was actually possible to feel the feathery villi lining the intestinal wall.

For years, this extraordinary scenario came back to her from time to time. It would be, she imagined, like running your palm and then fingertips across the underside of the starfish and the sea anemones in the Tidal Touch Pool at the aquarium—the very creatures those stern admonitions posted on the low glass sides of the exhibition were warning visitors not to handle. As if anyone coming to the touch pool longed to pick up rocks or seaweed. It was so obviously the anemones that offered up their tempting brushability; why were they there, if you weren't allowed to stroke them? The notion that expansive areas of a similar waving, velvety, living nap could reside, hidden, deep inside people had not exactly surprised Liz—she'd had Human Biology, grade 10— but never had she considered sex a kind of interior petting. It might feel, she thought, like touching a washcloth underneath the surface of the bathwater, but even softer, and tight around your wrist—a muscular cuff. Holding an octopus that grabbed you back in a fearsome, unchosen hug.

She forgot the book for a few years. Sometime before her wedding, that passage came back to her, with its idea that this was another definition of closeness. It still struck her as odd, the notion of having someone on your arm like a glove puppet. Intimate, obviously. *Intimate*.

At that time, Liz seemed to have reached a backstop in the level of closeness she foresaw in her marriage. She thought this was perhaps not the most hopeful sign, right beforehand. Getting ready to spend decades together, presumably through corporeal events like childbirth, accidents, illnesses (food poisoning; surgery; whatever else might come along), aging, infirmity, death, all with their various seepages and leaks; and already she had made up her mind: Beyond this I will not look, so don't ask me. I won't be going inside you.

Not, she believed then, pre-wedding, that she ought to feel guilty about her uninterest in massaging the epithelial lining of Stokes's colon. Just that maybe it would be prudent not to have her lifelong decisions made before the ceremony even took place. That it sounded wise to head into a marriage aware that there might be visceral things to attend to, someday. Growing old or dying, either way, would mean blood, mess, getting closer than you thought you could. Being willing to delve in there.

Liz got back to Ontario late on Tuesday, spent the night at her mother's hushed house, where she had left her car, and drove the next morning to the farm museum. Stokes was in his work clothes in the shingled office attached to the barn, making notes for the unstructured playground they had received a grant to build.

"There he is," she said. He felt so firm when she hugged him. Like a trout. "I missed you."

"Hey, I missed you more. It was boring here."

"I brought you some waffles Mom made this morning." She handed him a margarine container of warm waffle sticks and a mini jar of maple syrup, sticky on the outside. While he ate, she told him about the chuckwagon racing; the beef jerky competition they went to, one of many; the mechanical bull in the hotel lobby that she had urged Rena to ride, osteoporosis dangers notwithstanding. Rena refused but seemed to like being asked.

"Mom kept saying, 'It's just so different, everything's different.' She acted old, but we stayed busy."

"I'm glad," Stokes said. "She needed something like that."

"And what did you get up to? No affair while I was gone?"

He shook his head. "No affair. Netflix and potato chips."

"Well, that's a relief."

After years of never having semen inside her, she needed now to want it, desire it as wholesome. No squeamishness about stickiness, dampness. Years of containing had to be switched off. Receptiveness and welcome.

Sharing the Calgary hotel room with her mother, Liz had thought about Rena's words in the airport. Her mom's legs had gotten skinny and blue; her buttocks drooped down, without her floppy underpants, like unbaked biscuits. It had been so long since Liz had seen Rena change clothes. Her little breasts bagged down the front of her bony chest. All over, she was blotchy, discoloured, knobby, loose. And she wasn't even sick.

Liz would take care of Rena when she was dying, of course, but it was different from what Calvin had been lucky enough to have. One goes; one remains: math.

She thought of all the things she had known and forgotten, remembered again and forgotten again—all the weird facts and discoveries that kept disappearing and then washing ashore again. A few weeks before her father died, she was sitting in the room with him, keeping him company and not talking much.

"Wasn't I telling you about the eagle that watched me one time?" he asked. His voice was roughened but faint.

Liz nodded. "You were in the car, and the eagle was in a tree. And you stared at each other."

He said, "I was thinking, that's probably the most clearly I've ever been seen in my life."

Though it was far from the last time he spoke to her, that was the last story he told her. A story could be so short, she thought. Just a sentence, a line.

As she grows older, there seems to be more confusion inside her head about events from the past. She'll ask herself, *How long ago was that? Three years, ten years?* They seem equally plausible. The future, too, with the baby, the aging, the dying. Her or Stokes; fifty-fifty.

The mess is okay, she thinks. The blood is not so bad.

They Will Go to Loch Ness

Rebecca doesn't find it such a stretch that there could, maybe, possibly, be a Loch Ness monster. Malcolm, either. He often agrees with her, which is restful; her first husband, Wayne, only concurred with her on topics where he'd already taken a mental position, and hers happened to come along and coincide. Then he would acknowledge that he felt or thought the same way, though it was usually said grudgingly and with some declaration of how he had already staked out that intellectual territory a good while earlier. Wayne had never wanted to owe Rebecca anything.

Quite a tiring guy to live with.

Now, two decades on, it strikes her sometimes as so lucky and welcome to have landed with a man who can simply agree with her, who has no deep-seated dread of being influenced or persuaded by her opinions. *Thank you*, she'll murmur into the shower spray, or at the slapping windshield wipers; quick, private gratitude that she's here now: *Thank you. Thank you.* Her first husband wasn't the worst, she knows; it's just that this one's better. On television, the narrator in his little rowboat explains, "With a floor that's oddly smooth and flat, the lake drops away steeply from the bank. At this particular point, our boat is only sixty feet from shore, yet the water here goes down perhaps five hundred feet."

"Do you want popcorn?" she asks, moving the cat and rising.

"Sure," Malcolm says. "So what do you guess?"

"I don't see why not," she replies. "That's a ton of water."

"True," he says. Imagine: someone with whom it wasn't always a goddamn argument.

This show's focus is on the hoaxes and how they were perpetrated. For days afterwards Rebecca keeps thinking about it, homing in on one narrow aspect of the most famous hoax. It's the Surgeon's Photo from 1934, the one that shows a placid-looking, long-necked beast on the lapping surface. The toy monster had been constructed by modelmaker Christian Spurling, at the request of the photographer, the improbably named Marmaduke Wetherell. And then Spurling sat on that secret for sixty years, not admitting the truth until shortly before his death, age 93.

What an appalled Rebecca keeps mulling is that a little dose of fame could so corrupt a person's whole approach to life. It's the "on his deathbed" part that galls her—the notion that, even though decades had passed, that one incident and its resulting blare became the focus of the man's lifetime. His patchy little time of importance hadn't even been in the spotlight; he was near the interviews, but still anonymous.

To Rebecca, Spurling's late-life confession seems not just weirdly pitiable or ill-planned; her feeling about it is closer to contempt. What would it mean to your family, being shunted aside by a dying person who wanted to get in front of a camera and be talked about? His impulse, faced with death, was to explain a prank, and his friends, colleagues, wife and children—all of them count less than this weird tabloid story from decades earlier? The cheat itself is a cheat. Such a hollow trade, she's convinced, amounts to an announcement that the briefly famous person lacked even rudimentary self-knowledge.

Back in her childhood ballet years, Rebecca was fascinated by Anna Pavlova, the ballerina, who died of pneumonia in 1931 at age fifty and was still well known when Rebecca was young. It was said that in her final moments, Pavlova asked to hold the costume she'd worn for her most famous role, a cheerless solo called *The Dying Swan*. But if she wanted to rest her eyes on her white feathered tutu while her consciousness faded, did that mean she was thinking only of her fame? (Unwise as well as superficial, the critical and never-wrong twelve-year-old Rebecca thought.) Or had Pavlova's mind been on her work, which she loved deeply and had devoted her life to? (Defensible and understandable, judged Rebecca, lips pursed, assessing the life choices of a grown woman she was reading about in a second-rate ballet title written for children.)

That particular ballet mourned the evanescence of life, and here was Pavlova, not old but unexpectedly at the end—finding herself, no doubt to her disbelief, really cast as the swan that she had portrayed so many times on the stage. Out of all moments in the span of human history, Pavlova had the misfortune to develop pneumonia just a few years before antibiotics could have saved her. And now what she had practised so often was required of her.

Rebecca has also watched videos of a later ballerina, role inheritor Maya Plisetskaya, dancing Dying Swan; she doesn't seem human. With her arms bonelessly rippling up and down as she comes toward the audience out of an inky blackness, she looks like a stingray.

Rebecca's aunt Perce actually saw Plisetskaya perform that ballet in Wolfville, in 1972, when the Bolshoi Ballet did an improbable tour that landed them in Nova Scotia. (For young Rebecca it was an opportunity missed, one a tiny part of her still grieves. Why had her parents not bothered to get her there? Did they really not know what it would have meant to her?)

This is a professional lineage and heritage Pavlova was part of; she bequeathed the boneless-armed swan role, which had been choreographed for her, to Plisetskaya, who made it unforgettable. Involvement in such a project, a nearly transspecies artistic leap or similar rare achievement, seems different from sad Christian Spurling, fecklessly letting his life revolve around one secret that brought decades of fame and controversy crashing down (but in the wrong spot, accidentally leaving him anonymous). So, good fame and bad fame, is what she's thinking. Or, more accurately, legit fame and undignified fame.

Loser fame, with your life lived out merely in relation to what other people thought of it.

She doesn't believe she is better than Christian Spurling was; not exactly. More alive, perhaps. Certainly in possession of a keener sense of perspective. These are the arguments that get her ranting silently.

Ah, what do you care, she asks herself. Some stranger, now dead, did something foolish? Chasing fame is neither new, nor finished; look at that humiliating "balloon boy" hoax for reality TV. Some pitiful prairie family wanting their chance in front of a camera; how'd that work out? People waste their lives all the time, and who are you arguing with, anyway.

On the one hand: Feeling so superior is both wrong and irrelevant.

On the other: What makes people choose such a tragic lack of integrity?

And yet: Desiring fame for its own sake is not the worst choice a person could make. And isn't being judgy as bad as being dumb?

(No, she thinks. Not even close.)

After the fact, it's apparent that the thing had been rigged up from a swim toy. It's not only the blunt snout that should have been a giveaway, but also the bobbing, facile charm. Just popped up out of the water, like a periscope: *Ah, there she is.* No accident that Christian Spurling was, by trade, a skilled modelmaker—the execution of the neck and head is lifelike, wholly plausible.

She says to Malcolm, "It's funny, but it seems like a Nessie, if it did turn up now, would resemble the toy one. It's so iconic, it kind of crowds any other possibility out of your mind."

"Yeah, that's a guy who was good at his craft," he says.

"It's those little tufty sort of lumps at the top of the head that make it convincing," she says. "What would they be? The ears? Skull bones? They're really well done."

"I was thinking, it would be nice to go over to Scotland," Malcolm says. "Roam around some. We're about due for a trip."

"We are," she says. Rebecca is a nurse; planning time off is a hassle but always worth it. A little jolt of newness—that's what they need.

*   *   *

The lake isle poem, isn't that it? With the bee-loud glade, and something something bean rows. To live alone, like Thoreau. Yeats. No, wait; Yeats was Irish. She has confused the Loch Ness area with Innisfree, in, she realizes, some ignorant North American conflation of Scotland with Ireland. The wild swans at Coole. Inverness; that's it. Totally different. But whatever; some peaceful place with a lake and brisk good weather and no one to bother you.

That "whatever" is rude, of course, if unvoiced thoughts can be rude. Though she now lives in Toronto, which everyone has heard of, she recalls how annoyed people used to get with Americans, whose maps rarely included eastern Canada. This left them unfortunately prone to thinking there was nothing east of Maine until you hit Europe. Explaining where she lived back then could feel like saying she had grown up in the Bermuda Triangle: a doubtful, possibly non-existent place.

In any case, she would like to stand in Scotland, carefully balancing on slippery grey rocks, and look out over the steep-sided lake. Hear lapping, right at her feet. Chilly enough to need a jacket, even in July. Not waiting for anything to happen; just watching. As the documentary explained, so much peat, in fine, fine particles, washes into the lake from the area's streams that visibility in the water is low. That's been part of the trouble with the hunt over the decades.

Rebecca's heart goes out to an imaginary Nessie, both lonely and at rest, concealed from all her searchers by the infinitesimal suspended particles in this dim brown world, while slow, peaceful raindrops fall from the grey sky. Thinks of knowing only water.

She remembers spinning the globe that sat on the dining room sideboard when she was young. Tracing her finger across the ocean to France, wondering if a French girl was tracing westward and trying to picture Rebecca.

"I like your idea of going to Scotland," she says on the weekend. They have taken overseas trips three times together; Iceland, Portugal, India. They usually travel every few years and have been saving up for a while now, but it doesn't need to be soon. "Just sometime," she says. "Not right away."

"Sounds good," Malcolm says. He was in Scotland once, fifty years ago, visiting elderly relatives with his father, people he was never in touch with again and can't remember. "I can find out where my great-grandfather lived, in Glasgow, and maybe we can walk around his neighbourhood."

"Great," she says. Malcolm is seventy-four; they probably shouldn't put it off forever. Insurance for travellers becomes exorbitant once you hit eighty; hasn't she read that? And there are other trips she vaguely hopes to fit in: Thailand, New Zealand. Belize, maybe.

* * *

Malcolm tells her things she finds interesting, but he doesn't lecture and he doesn't explain. And he usually passes the test of not telling her things she's likely to know.

As in the other day, when he passed along an insight he read about cats and closed doors: They're not forgetting they were just in there; rather, they're patrolling. Now Rebecca regards Lucia, with her ceaseless meowing to be admitted to or released from a room, in a different light. Lucia's not complaining; she's just trying to do her job.

It's pleasurable, getting new perspectives in this way. Such attributes, Rebecca considers, offset their age difference. Or part of it, anyway. Say twelve years' worth.

Then there's the fact that Malcolm seldom repeats himself. That's worth another five years of age-gap-closing points, she thinks.

And the remaining five years; what will she say balances that? His housework approach, perhaps—the way he tackles the indoor stuff so automatically, not assuming that his domain is the time-flexible list of outdoor tasks among which a person can pick and choose as the mood strikes: *Oh, I think I feel like cleaning out the gutters today.* Then, la la la, *Hmm, maybe I'll knock off now and have a beer.*

There, Rebecca thinks. That's the whole twenty-two-year age gap accounted for. He's still an entire generation older than she is; but in legitimate, meaningful ways, it can seem reduced to zero.

*   *   *

She's been unkind toward Christian Spurling; her prissy disdain was misguided. Malcolm sets her straight. Rebecca didn't see the whole program.

"No, it wasn't like that," Malcolm tells her now. "Not some final confession. It was that these two guys, journalists, tracked Spurling down to learn more about that photo. They found him and asked him about it, and so he told them the truth. I didn't get the impression his life had revolved around being associated with it."

"Really?" she asks him. "Are you sure?" It's so at odds with her mental picture of the deathbed scene—the truth coming out as the man's life telescopes down to one line connecting two moments, with nothing else in between them. She tries to rejig her idea of how it happened, but that's hard. As it turns out, the hoax had been a way to get back at a tabloid. Which seems perfectly reasonable. "You really don't think he established his life around it? For me, that was the most interesting aspect."

So Spurling and Wetherell found the thing got away from them, the way a prank will; the way a misdemeanor can become a felony as seamlessly as if that had been the plan. Something starts and you can't back out. Or, rather, with every day that passes you see that you could have recanted, if only you'd done it a little sooner. That's the trap, Rebecca thinks: the constant feeling of having just rushed past the point of no return, and then the remorse-heavy knowledge that trails behind.

It wasn't too late yesterday, but it's too late now.

And tomorrow, with conviction: Oh, it *wasn't* too late yesterday; but it's too late now.

Persuasive; but wrong. Seeming true doesn't make it true.

*   *   *

"How's your ancient partner?" Rebecca's mother, Kate, asks her on the phone.

"Still alive," Rebecca says. It's a tiny bit funny; mostly not. Predictable. Malcolm is four years younger than

Kate. Rebecca's father has been dead long enough that he doesn't figure into her reckoning; but if he were here, he'd be three years older than Malcolm. Rebecca, when she was thirty-eight and divorced and sure she would never meet anyone again, hadn't been paying attention.

Malcolm's arrival into Rebecca and Kate's relationship had surprising effects from the start. The first Christmas, one of Kate's gifts to them was a citrus juicer—a small pitcher with a rotating reamer on top. It had crevices where pulp got caught, and cleaning it required patient stints with a toothpick under running water.

"This is ridiculous," Malcolm said, the third time she tried to make use of it. "Throw the thing away."

Rebecca agreed to get rid of it but hoped to donate it somewhere. That trailing cord, she realized, was fooling her, making the juicer look like a helpful appliance that surely someone would need.

"Honey, it's garbage; nobody wants it," he said. "Toss it."

Throwing it away created a flick of remorse that, surprisingly, converted instantly to relief, like blue litmus paper turning pink. Still, Rebecca didn't expect Malcolm to tell Kate, when she asked about it on a visit.

"Oh, we had to let that one go, Katie," he said, dexterously not quite saying Rebecca had finally dropped it in the trash. He was casual, peer to peer. "The lid would get clogged with pulp, and we couldn't get it clean again."

Kate said only, "Oh, too bad," and that it had been on sale at Target, and moved on. And her casual acceptance had widened to include Rebecca, as well.

It was as if, Rebecca thought, her own age was now being averaged with Malcolm's, and she had miraculously gained a half-generation of credibility that she could make use of whenever she needed to. Which wasn't a bad swap for being in a type of relationship she'd always found suspect, before she met him.

Back then, post-divorce but pre-Malcolm, she'd taken extension classes, two every semester. Not even trying to meet someone; just filling her evenings. Upholstery; anthropology; cake decorating; basic astronomy. An algebra refresher course, cheese making, jazz.

*   *   *

At some point it comes to her: There's one extra thing she wants. More time. More life; *another* life.

And of course this is one upside of being with Malcolm. No matter what else she knows, she's almost certain of that one fact—he'll die someday; she will still be here. As bleak as that time seems—and already those long years of grief press down on her, anticipating— she will, nonetheless, get another chance. A future will fan out again, and she'll have options, a wide meadow. She might someday, improbably, own that condo in the middle of a city, as she's always wished.

It's hard to fathom that, at fifty-two, she's still unsure what lies ahead. That time after Malcolm is her life in reserve, her extended grace period. She might marry for a third time; she could fall in love with a woman. She might move to Vancouver. Learn to ski.

You couldn't say that someone would reason it out that way, in deciding to start a relationship with an older man. Looking years, even decades, into the future; thinking of the end of a life, and afterward. Though Rebecca has concluded over the years that her mind is craftier, a more wide-ranging planner, than she acknowledges in her daily life. Yet who would be so calculating? Who would opt for a planned widowhood? (Still, she must have known. She can count. She can subtract.)

*   *   *

She doesn't realize it, but being wrong about Christian Spurling's motive isn't the limit of her wrongness in the Nessie department. When Rebecca starts fooling around with airline ticket prices, she's not expecting to see a monster on a Scottish lake but also not aware that she has misunderstood the odds. She thought they were slim; in fact, they were zero. She missed the end of the show, with its debunking of possibility.

Nessie seems plausible because Loch Ness is huge. That was the thinking explored in the first half of the documentary, the part Rebecca bought into. It's twenty-three miles long; seven hundred fifty feet deep. It holds more water than all the lakes in England and Wales combined. Why wouldn't a strange, vast occupant glide around down there? Look at the creatures turning up regularly in the oceans that have never been seen before: Life is always popping up in places where biologists have declared nothing could live.

But the second half, explaining that Loch Ness is too cold to harbour reptiles; and the region was under a mile-thick layer of ice until only eighteen thousand years ago; and the lake holds just twenty-two tons of fish, which would not support plesiosaur-sized creatures— Rebecca heard none of that.

Of course, this is not so unusual: to be more wrong than you know. To be even more wrong than the considerably

and shamingly wrong you grapple with being half the
time anyway. It was a clarifying opportunity missed—
don't just watch the first half and think you grasp the
whole picture; that would be the lesson, distilled. But
Rebecca didn't catch it; it flew by her, unheeded, in the
way of so many insights and truths that could improve
our lives if we noticed them.

Yet what does it matter? Somehow, over the insom-
niac weeks of that steady Toronto August, the thought
of sliding through water like that ancient, elongated animal helps Rebecca fall asleep. There's a Nessie hunter
guy living in a van on the shore of Loch Ness who
believes the search is on now for the last one or two
of their species—that the gap of time for spotting them
is about to slam shut. Rebecca won't let herself dwell on
the heartrending aspects of being the last survivor, but
she does find it calming to imagine swimming, huge and
self-contained, in that brown water, guarding peace at
her deep heart's core. Plisetskaya, moving forward out of
blackness, arms dipping and rising like dainty fins moving her through water. On the shore of sleep, Rebecca
ponders, with what drowsy attention she can muster,
all the time that lies ahead—reaches her mind into the
future, a million years, four million years, when she herself will have become their skinny little ossified Lucy figure, a tiny, primitive person who hadn't known much.

She imagines everything, everyone, shifted into the
past. She thinks of the Sumerians, replaced by the Akka-
dians, who were followed by the Babylonians. In Niger,
the Tenerian people lived a thousand years after the
Kiffian people and buried their dead in the same spot.
She thinks of her planet so changed—its blue-green eye
become one she herself would not recognize, and her

satisfying lifetime pushed so far in the past it's rendered meaningless.

She imagines things left behind, gone forever: coffee, planes, plastic, zoos; North America gone, and western civilization not just vanished but covered over. Gone: elastic; nail polish; nuts and bolts. Cheese, maybe wheat, dissolved into an ancient and unknowable history. No more pens, wrenches, I-beams, cable-spool coffee tables. No race for the White House; no White House. People who had somehow outlived electronics, surgery, stock markets, written language, engines. She tries to list and imagine the deaths of the old arts—whittling, quilting, canning—and then those things that seem sure to last: intoxication, maybe. International trade. Hot baths. As long as there's water, she tells herself, people will heat it up and get in it.

She lay lightly on the mattress, waiting for sleep. She rested by the man she would probably outlive. She rested like an insect on her tiny bead of time.

The Golden Bra

When I finally stole a look inside my sister Hayden's refrigerator, I was startled. Much had changed in the way of healthy-food-sounding alcohol. Hayden was basically doing her grocery shopping at the liquor store. She had coffee ale, presumably for mornings; apricot IPA and plum porter, I guess for her produce needs; pecan beer (her version of Southern cooking), and lemon hard cider; there's your vitamin C. Also chocolate stout.

"What are you looking for?" she demanded.

"Is there any way at all that I can help you with your drinking?" I asked, closing the fridge door very very gently, as if I hadn't quite taken in what I'd just seen. That's my last-ditch way of dealing with her: try to be frank but also leave a little escape clause in there.

"Paige, I do not have a problem. I have been extremely clear with you about that. On the other hand, *you* unquestionably have a problem with trying to control my life," she said—her standard reply to my muted annual or biannual declaration that she was out of control.

She always stayed on message, and the message was that opting for beer rather than coffee when she woke up was not odd, because our mom's dementia and the stress of her caretaking were creating understandable extra drinking that would taper off, with no effort on Hayden's part, when things got easier. Presumably after our mother died, which her doctors were saying could be a long time indeed.

Twenty years earlier, on Thanksgiving, I had watched Hayden nearly burn the sweet potato pie and then, evidently rattled by the magnitude of this near-tragedy, down a tall glass of Ravenswood zinfandel, like a child finishing her milk in order to leave the table. Of course I'd seen people drink beer that way, but it was startling to watch someone slam back a twelve-ounce tumbler of wine. Her eyes cut over toward me from the side, with her throat lifted and the glass tipped all the way. She was watching me watch her, and she wasn't trying to hide. It was as if the lack of surreptitiousness could make it normal.

"Look, this is insane. You've really, truly got a drinking problem," I said then, jarred nearly much by the essentially private nature of what I'd just witnessed as by the size of the glass. It was the first time I tried to talk with her about it.

"I do not," she said reflexively, as if she'd been waiting for me to say something. "Plenty of people these days use water glasses for wine."

"They don't inhale it like cigarette smoke," I said. "It would be even faster if you just stuck a straw in the bottle. Carried around an IV pole."

That was probably eight thousand bottles of wine ago.

Spending more time with her now, one development I saw was that hand in hand with the drinking went her lying. She did it automatically, to me and to our younger sister, Carlin; to each of us individually or both of us together, on any topic or pretext. It didn't have to be about our mother or her needs or anything with the house. She lied as a means of self-protection, to stock-pile a little time or credit, to gain a few points that she might or might not need later; she did it to throw up a cloud of words and fuzz and confusion that might have no immediate purpose or benefit while she was talking, but, who knew, could come in handy sometime. She lied because it was a skill she still had, perhaps something that made her feel competent or gave her a sense of privacy.

Our mother lived for another two years after I saw the fridge of liquor groceries, and Hayden was her care-giver—a symbiotic relationship that meant she could stop pretending to job hunt altogether, and she felt entitled to budget the household money however she chose. She moved the two of them into a small rented bungalow close enough to all necessary stores that she rarely had to drive.

Carlin and I tried to make changes, but our mom seemed to be receiving decent care, albeit from an alcoholic. Hayden might go to bed early, but I also saw how gentle she was.

"Let's get you set up here in your big chair," she'd say, clucking around with shawls and footstools. "You want a snack? Want some of those fig cookies you like, with some lemonade?"

Our mother was washed and fresh-smelling, dry inside her diaper, wearing her special stockings to keep the swelling down. Hayden cooked Mom's scrambled eggs the way she liked them, and she popped the tricky denture plate out deftly, then patted her on the cheek. Yes, Hayden was a slow-moving crisis, but the truth was that she never had a DUI and wouldn't get behind the wheel of a car when she'd had a drink. (This was one of the sources of her employment problems.) Why should she listen to us?

She'd turfed Carlin out, when she moved home from Arizona with no money and no place to stay; but Carlin, who was mad for a long time, had gotten over it.

"No, I wouldn't want to move back in there," Carlin said. "I was always more conflicted about living with Mom than Hayden is. Besides, I've made a new life now." She was even talking about maybe dating again— not that she had signed up for Plenty of Older Fish or whatever, but her attitude shift was healthy.

So we made an uneasy peace with having our mother in Hayden's hands. Two different doctors told me that alcoholics could sometimes be excellent caregivers. And if we were to step in, where would Hayden go?

Nine months after our mother died I was trying to figure out where things stood with her estate. Hayden had all the paperwork and was not making it easy. When she answered the phone (not often; she has always preferred to be the one making the calls), she stalled.

"I really need to see the paperwork," I'd say.

"And I'm going to be able to show you that, very soon. I'm just waiting on a couple more documents from her lawyer, and that will be the last of what I need. I've been going through her papers—you know what a mess those are—and getting everything in order, and I expect to have it finished this week."

"So by Friday, you mean?"

"Yes, definitely by Friday. I'm nearly finished now; I'm just waiting on these last few documents. I'll call the lawyer's office this morning and make sure they've been sent out."

"Huh. Definitely by Friday, is what you're saying."

"Yes. I will not let you down on this."

This is the thing: She could straight-up deliver the bullshit, but because she was not precisely lying, it was impossible to call her on it. I was never sure whether she believed the slippery nonsense she spouted, or things had just gotten so foggy in her head that she didn't know what she was claiming. Plus, one small part of me (the part that should be attending Al-Anon) held out the hope that perhaps this time she would come through.

Who promises, "I will not let you down on this?" Boyfriends who are about to break up with you. People with early-stage dementia, who think they can still handle a project they can no longer manage. Gamblers. Lying coworkers. And family members who drink. Saying "I won't let you down" is a promise: "I still love you; you're important to me; I honour and value our relationship." All the sentiments I still craved in our relationship.

That's what we had come to. Wanting to believe my older sister still loved me now made me a sucker and a fool, vaguely pathetic and puppy-like, unable to learn from experience. I felt like a high-school girl reluctant to let go of her first boyfriend. An objective observer would say, "Why do you keep chasing this relationship?"

Because it was so much harder than I ever imagined to quit hoping.

When we were in our forties, a change took place in the way Hayden responded to news items from me. I noticed it one day when I told her I was thinking of taking harp lessons. This whimsical idea had come to me at a Christmas concert that had seemed to wrap peace and compassion in a soft blanket of notes.

"Oh, you're psychic," Hayden said. "I'm going to begin harp lessons myself, in the new year, with a teacher from Italy who's at the college this year." Though, as far as I know, she never did.

For that matter, I didn't, either. It was a passing thought.

And she had these wild notions. "Chuck and I are going to start making and selling mozzarella. We're going to raise buffalo." This was before he disappeared from the scene.

"Buffalo, for real? Aren't they, I don't know, hard to keep fenced? I've heard they're always getting loose."

"Not if you take the time to figure out what you're doing. They're just big cattle, and people raise cattle all the time."

Then, "I'm in touch with Russ Feingold's office on some projects Sy Hersh had indicated an interest in writing about." Hayden had been a paralegal at a law firm that represented a number of whistleblowers— persecuted heroes she strongly identified with.

"Oh, what kind of projects?"

"Well, I can't tell you yet; I'll be able to discuss more details in a couple of weeks."

Trying to identify the smidgen of truth at the heart of these stories was a fool's errand, I finally realized. Just reaching that simple understanding took me years upon years. In the meantime, I continued mostly falling for it—doubtful; expressing surprise; but still somehow persuaded that Hayden would not just make shit up as a matter of course. I was still miscalculating the amount of respect that remained between us.

I wanted her to stop the guzzling, sure; but mostly I wanted to feel that she was going to be all right. She didn't have enough people in her life—basically me, Carlin, and a polite neighbour who helped her out with Mom for eight dollars an hour when Hayden needed backup. All I could see ahead was fog and fear.

"Look, Hayden, you need to be going to AA meetings. I can go with you to some if it would be helpful. Do you think that would make it easier for you?"

"Listen to me. I understand what causes my problems, and it's not my drinking."

"Oh, really. Being drunk from the time you wake up at lunchtime until you crash on the sofa and fall asleep in your clothes at three a.m. is not a problem."

"My problem has always been related to security. So, for instance, if it's a situation where I'm insecure about money, I get scared and panicky, and then I drink more. It's a response to anxiety."

"Okay. And, in the meantime, so you can get back into a job, you would benefit from going back to a few AA meetings."

"They weren't right for me. They weren't convenient, and they weren't a good fit."

"Not con*ven*ient—for god's sake; there's a meeting every hour in every part of town, seven days a week; they couldn't get any more convenient. I'll drive you right to the door and go in with you and fix your coffee, cream and one sugar. I'll sit there and chat to people with you. I won't try to make you feel ashamed. I just want you to get better, Hayden. Trying to handle this by yourself hasn't worked for you. Do you remember enough about normal life to know that most people do not in fact start drinking first thing in the morning, and that it's pretty shocking to be in a state where your life has come to that?"

"This is a temporary thing, first with the stress over Mom and taking care of her, and now settling her paperwork and her accounts. I know I've been drinking more than usual, but that's just because the situation is unusual. I'm not concerned. I'll be back in a regular routine when things slow down a bit with all the legal stuff."

When she was in maybe sixth grade and I was in fourth, the Cato's clothing store in our small downtown displayed a gold lamé bikini in their front window. Hayden and I loved that thing. We called it the G.B., the Golden Bra, and talked to each other about where we would wear it, how sexy our imaginary future husbands would find us in it. That brazen shininess of it was something we'd never seen—the three triangles, and the way they pulled your eyes straight to the relevant areas. We never called it the G.B. & P.; we didn't realize it was a bikini rather than underwear. Displaying it was, for us, like showing the mannequins having sex right there in the store window on Main Street. Even television was so chaste then—before *Charlie's Angels*, way before reality TV. The Golden Bra was a promise that fully adult lives lay ahead for us. There would be all kinds of choices ahead, and we would be able to make them happen.

Neither Carlin nor I had ever comprehended the extent and ferocity of Hayden's problem.

"The future looks really bad," Carlin told me.

"You know what? I think it's already here. Her future happened a long time ago, in her twenties and thirties and forties," I said. "How could she make it different now?"

"When did she start drinking? Do you know?" Carlin asked.

"She got suspended for three days in tenth grade for getting drunk on a field trip," I said. "That's the first time I remember. When I got in from school that day, no one else was home yet, and she was clearing bottles out of her bedroom and pouring them down the sink. She had them hidden in coat pockets and florists' boxes in the back of her closet, and she got me to help her find them all and get rid of them before Mom and Dad got home and the school called." Those long boxes with skeletal dried roses in them, the petals turned brown and crisp. Pint gin bottles nestled down under the fraying dried greenery. I helped Hayden try to find them all—it was like our Easter egg hunts from childhood; we kept overlooking places on the first couple of passes—and then she took the empty bottles out to the back yard and hid them under the kudzu vines at the edge of our property, to retrieve later, after she had faced our parents with her story and given them a few days to settle down.

"I don't remember that," Carlin said.

"You were really young still. So you'd only hear about it later."

"I don't remember hearing about it at all."

"Yeah, maybe not," I said, and for the first time it seemed odd to me that our parents wouldn't have told Carlin about Hayden's problems—that even within our immediate family, discussing it was too difficult or forbidden. Our parents were fond of the path of least discomfort. I remember how the bottles clinked as Hayden and I poured them out and flung the empties out into the tangle of vines. "Rum" and "vodka" and "gin" had been just unfamiliar words to me. I babysat for families who sometimes had wine or beer, nothing more. How had Hayden, at fifteen, smuggled all this new vocabulary into the house without any of us knowing about it?

"She hid her yearbook from Mom and Dad, because so many of her friends wrote their messages 'to Haydencoholic.' I remember Mom kept asking to see it. Hayden kept saying she'd left it at school."

"Imagine that as your nickname," Carlin said. "In high school."

Hayden phoned my mom one afternoon eight years ago and said she was being checked into a hospital, there in Scottsdale, into the psychiatric ward. She was too out of it to give more information, and she didn't answer her phone after that. We phoned our way down a list of hospitals around Scottsdale to find her. She was having seizures, by then, from alcohol withdrawal; after a few days they said she was stable, and Carlin flew out to empty her apartment, clear out her storage unit, and bring her back, unemployable, broke, and in a rage.

Carlin, recently divorced, had been living with Mom and taking care of her, but it made sense for Hayden to take on that role. Carlin bought a condo. Hayden got dug in, I see now, like a tick, though that wasn't apparent at the time. (Sensible and kind all around, we agreed. Let Hayden begin her recovery in a peaceful, health-promoting atmosphere; Mom would have companionship and a Sudoku partner, for as long as she could still do Sudoku.) Hayden had fled Arizona with no forwarding address, as far as Carlin and I could tell, since no hospital bills ever reached us; but that didn't seem like our fight to take on.

It was a bad sign. Why had I never known about Hayden that she hung onto all the money she possibly could?

After three weeks, she texted for a drive to another medical appointment. I went over there with Carlin, to discuss Hayden's health, and that was when we learned what she'd been up to.

"I had power of attorney, and I needed to make some adjustments, which were fully justified and were required, in order to keep our mother comfortable and safe in her final months. I would have included you in this planning, but it was such a hectic and disordered time that it needed to be handled as expeditiously and smoothly as possible. Mom trusted me with her affairs, and so I naturally made the judgment call that needed to be made."

"But you're not entitled to everything."

"You'll find that any lawyer or judge would be fully acquiescent with my having used my judgment to make necessary decisions. There's no question that I needed to be compensated for my years of taking care of her. She did not want to go into a nursing home, and she didn't have to. Obviously some retroactive caregiver compensation for those duties, paid by the estate, is fully in line with legal precedent and understanding."

"You're telling us you changed the will."

"I am not telling you that, and you are making slanderous statements. I'm telling you it is quite clearly not just legitimate but expected that I be compensated by the estate for my years of caregiving."

"She had dementia! You can't get her to change her will! Hayden, the only reason you're living here rent-free, taking care of her, is because you are completely unemployable and desperate. It was charity." I was getting loud.

"Her doctors are in agreement with me that her mental faculties were intact at the time these decisions were made."

"I cannot believe I'm hearing this. I really cannot believe what you are saying." My legs and my hands were trembling; even my feet seemed to tremble. *You are sick, sick, sick,* I was thinking. Silas, her spookily quiet pit bull pug mix, came tiptoeing in, nosing the air in his sinister way, and I pictured him registering my rage and going for my throat.

Carlin and I left, me thinking I might have an aneurism. I walked home from Carlin's, fantasizing about poisoning, electrocution.

Email went unanswered, and she wouldn't pick up the phone. The only reply was a text saying, "You have indicated that you have counsel. Communicate with me through your counsel."

I had indeed made an appointment with a lawyer, but it didn't go well. He told me that we needed to put this behind us and find a way to get along. I was filled with shame. I'd never had anything but contempt for families who fought over wills.

Carlin and I diverged. She wanted to move on; there hadn't been all that much money and Hayden had no doubt spent it all anyway. I thought that was beside the point, that she shouldn't get away with blatant theft.

I hated Hayden, tearing me from Carlin, even. I kept thinking, *There's not going to be anything left of our family before all this is finished.* We were it; we were the last three.

"It didn't seem as bad when it wasn't our money she was spending," Carlin said, and I agreed. It sounded awful of us but was kind of true; Hayden's destroying herself from the inside was even worse with our money.

"I feel like she's finished," Carlin said one day.

"Yeah," I said. "She spent her potential a long time ago. Then she burned through her resources."

"And then she squandered her inheritance from Grandma," Carlin said. "And now she's spending ours."

"That's about the size of it," I said. "She doesn't know any other way to live her life. She's been drunk since she was a teenager. I don't think she could learn to function in the world now."

The silence from Hayden continued, which was always ominous. It usually meant she was plotting something. That, or about to be hospitalized again.

Grudgingly, ruefully, I decided I should drive over there and check on things. Make sure she was alive.

Hayden ran out of her house, brandishing her phone, yelling at me, "I'm filming! This is on camera!"

"Ah, Christ," I said, and called Carlin. "I'm over at Hayden's. I'm about to kill her."

"She's making trouble?"

"She's running around outside with her fucking phone, filming me and screeching about how she's documenting everything for her lawsuit."

"This is the last thing I need this morning," Carlin said. "Is she dressed?'

"Well, kind of," I said. "Everything but a shirt."

Church Vampires

Cathy had moved up to the Senior Youth Group now, the high-schoolers. Finally it was her turn on the haunted house work crew.

Her brother Bill advised, "Sign up as soon as Renee announces it. The first year I was old enough, I waited too long, and all the slots got taken."

"How many people does she have?"

"Maybe ten or twelve, depending. You become a tight group. That's what makes it fun." Bill was at UT Memphis now, studying to be a male nurse, except he just said a nurse. He had a not-too-dinged-up Oldsmobile Omega, and a drawer of L.L. Bean ragg pullovers, and a petite girlfriend named Molly to steam up his car windows with when he brought her to Chattanooga for a weekend. Bill's church days were behind him. But Cathy remembered, from observing his high-school seasons on the work crew, all the evidence that significant events went on amid the hammering and painting.

The haunted house was one of the youth group's main annual fundraisers, providing the biggest chunk of the money toward their year-end trip—to the Georgia mountains to see the European-village streets in Helen, still decorated for Christmas; or over to North Carolina to tour the holiday lights in McAdenville. Some short but meaningful excursion that would get the kids out of their parents' hair for a couple of days and give the group an opportunity for fellowship and reflection on the past twelve months. Maybe set some goals for the year to come, if there was time. Finding a way to pay for the excursions was important because Renee, their energetic youth leader, believed the teens would stop attending if church got un-fun.

The following Wednesday evening, during announcements, Renee indicated the sign-up sheet on the bulletin board by the Youth Kitchenette, and Cathy slipped over there during break. A bite-marked pencil dangled from a ratty string. At school she would have joined up with a friend, two friends, but here she was still looking for her clan; the people she used to hang out with had stopped coming. The list had Emily, Ember, Paul, Alan J., Alan R., Helena. She didn't know any of them well, and most were older. Emily Morrison went to the other school; she was always losing a contact lens, which halted activity while everyone searched the floor until it was located. Ember had hair she could sit on and was popular, in a self-contained, older-seeming way. Paul and Alan R. she didn't know much about, except that they had recently learned to drive a standard and they talked about stock car racing and Andre the Giant. Helena had written a one-person play, *Her Concealed Ventricle*, and performed it to acclaim at the All-Church Banquet the previous spring.

Alan J., though. Alan Randall Jordan. What she knew about him was scanty but sufficient. She admired even the bumps and contours of the letters of his name, as if she'd traced it out in the dark with a sparkler. On the margins of her homework she drew small roofline streetscapes that held his name like some medieval secret, with the high peak of the initial A making the tower of a fancy church in her tiny penciled town. She also liked his house's street number: 5118, a paradigm of elegance, deft near-symmetry, and a sort of witty, intentional completion, that 8 closing with a flourish. She liked his light Levi's, and the veins that stood out on his forearms, and his tender-looking earlobes. She didn't want to date Alan, exactly—too scary—but she would have put herself through almost anything to stand as close to him as she could reasonably get. That was the point at which her imagination switched from the physical to an unarticulated, unspecified longing.

Every other Wednesday, the second hour of the meeting was Games Night, and the youth had an ongoing tussle with Renee over what was permitted.

"Let's play Twister!" somebody always yelled, but Renee never gave in, even though she'd finally agreed to their bobbing for apples at the Haunted House Open House. Two people on opposite sides of a barrel of water, hands clasped behind their backs, mouths open above the water, trying to capture apples that were as evasive as if they had minds. The previous Youth Leader had let them play it but only one at a time, which missed the point. ("Renee, it's no fun if there's just one person!" "Okay, okay, but no more than two." Two was okay with them; two was the whole idea.)

"C'mon, Renee! What's wrong with Twister? We played it at birthday parties when we were little! It's fine!"

"Or strip poker!" That was Paul.

Renee wouldn't be drawn. "You guys," she'd say mildly. "You know why we don't play Twister anymore. Let's see, we've got Yahtzee, chess, Chinese checkers, dominoes, Connect Four."

That was the dynamic during any Youth event: various kids trying to introduce at least the potential for salacious developments, with Renee tirelessly patrolling the fence lines. On commercials, Twister was represented as some sort of family game, when clearly it wasn't for families. All that stretching and reaching; all those "*Whoops!* Dang! How did *that* happen" accidents.

Sometimes Renee brought in her old Mystery Date game board from home and casually established mixed groups. Shouty flirting ensued, but nothing actionable.

During the weeks of Haunted House construction, presumably there would be more than the usual opportunities for fumbling, nearness, someone else's breath or shoulder against your skin. Sitting briefly on someone's lap. None of it had to mean anything. Cathy understood this partly from remarks she'd overheard in previous autumns or things her brother had said, but mostly by osmosis. Construction involved not only shadowy passages and corridors, curtains, unsupervised minutes—places and times when things might unroll in unexpected ways—but also one afternoon following another, a period of getting to know people better every day. It was like a Biodome.

It all depended on who signed up. She had followed through on her plan: Alan Jordan had put his name down, and she had gathered her courage and done the same. She was committed.

And at the perimeter of her attention was a different, luxurious spaciousness—an awareness that, somehow, even Alan didn't have to matter so much. Yes, she loved him; he was why she was here. Yet there were other cute guys around, as well. (Or not even cute, exactly. Cute wasn't the prerequisite.) The potential lay more in the situation than in the individuals, who were, if not interchangeable, certainly an intriguing collection of overlapped near-futures, a bunch of roads diverging in a yellow wood, every one of them bristling with possibility.

There were complex rules for the Haunted House, and all the institutional memory lay with Renee. She knew that the youth group had long since concluded that no animals, alive or fake, should be part of the displays, because dead people could be funny-scary but cats or dogs were not. She remembered when they had last raised admission fees, and by how much, and the effect on total revenues. She easily recalled who was willing to loan them silver-plated candelabra to sit on top of the piano in the room where the vampire rose, groaning, in his casket; she could explain the sequence of steps for constructing the labyrinthine path that wound through the "rooms" and made the area seem bigger than it was.

The previous few years the Haunted House had included a jail cell, a pharmacy, a funeral parlour, a snake-infested school room, and a deadly picnic. Leon Bass, one of the ushers, always loaned the youth group his vintage Beetle: it was narrow enough to be pushed slowly through the French doors and parked in the Gillis Annex, where most big fundraising projects took place. The Volkswagen was then festooned with rubber arms and feet sticking out of the windows and hood.

Construction started right up on Monday, and when she arrived at four (having walked over from the school as slowly as possible, filled up with excitement and dread) everyone else was bustling around, looking enviably occupied. She was extra, exposed and raw.

She asked some guy, Nathan something, who was dashing past with a clipboard, "What should I do?"

He asked, "Do you want to build, paint, get props? Make costumes? Because we're changing up the rooms and characters this year."

"Paint," she said, since that seemed doable and maybe tantalizingly messy, in the laughter-filled way she kept picturing. Splashing paint around was something a fun girl in a commercial would do. While wearing short shorts.

"Painting, right," said Nathan, scribbling on his clipboard. "Go find Mitch MacDonald and his crew, and tell them you're going to help them."

This was worrying, in that Mitch was giant, with a woolly blond beard. He drove an El Camino he'd rebuilt himself and seemed more like a foreman than a student. Cathy had certainly never spoken to him, or planned to. Alan Jordan was thin and quick and rode a bicycle around town.

Nathan grinned at her. "Wrong guy to work with?"

She blushed scarlet. "I can do whatever," she said stiffly. "I don't care." Did he somehow know? About Alan?

"Well, they do need painters now, so you'll be useful there. We'll probably all do other stuff later on."

Cathy headed for the Annex, humiliation ticking inside her almost audibly.

When she approached the painters and told them, in a near-whisper, "Nathan said I should come help you guys out," they looked at her briefly and Mitch said, "Okay, but we don't need you yet." The boys were so large, their paint cans looked light. Cathy sat on the stairs for an hour doing algebra problems, and then it was getting toward dinnertime and she sidled out to the parking lot to meet her mom. Decades later, when Cathy was looking through a photo album of those years, she had a clear memory of Mitchell MacDonald, a hammer hanging from the loop of his painter's pants, raising a sheet of drywall with a clever tool he'd rigged up from a length of plumbing pipe and a few loops of wire. Everyone said it would make him wealthy. She didn't know; perhaps it had.

That beard. Like a lion's ruff.

The new minister's wife, Caroline Dunagan, had sent the youth group a sweet letter not long before her family arrived in Chattanooga, saying she was excited about the move to Tennessee and was looking forward to getting to know them all.

She had signed it "Mrs. Jerry Dunagan," which no one thought was that weird even though it was 1980. The final generation of women who used both their husbands' first and last names was on its way out. Caroline Dunagan, a young woman in her thirties, was unusual in doing so; it made her seem older than she was, and intimidatingly formal and correct.

"Renee, are you going to sign your husband's first name like that when you get married? Or do you think it's old-fashioned?" a high-school senior named Mandy had asked, one night when they were redecorating a bulletin board.

"I'm not sure I'll even change my name if I get married," Renee said. "I like the way it sounds now. Besides, isn't it kind of weird, not knowing what last name you'll get?" It was a notion simple enough to resonate. Cathy thought Renee did have a great last name: Callaway. A rich sound, like some kind of dessert. For most girls, there were years left before they encountered many married women who had kept their own last names. (And for a long time yet, retaining your name would seem rude and judgmental, a passive-aggressive device for scolding other people.)

But of course Caroline was lovely, when they met her in person. She promised to drop by Youth Group on Sundays to pop popcorn, and she went around telling everyone, "Call me Caro."

Her husband, the newly ensconced Reverend Jerry, was likewise kind of young (also kind of cute), and all the girls wanted him to think well of them. He said their group had tremendous potential and that Renee had clearly done great things. With more to come, he said.

His second week on the job, he finally got a full tour of the under-construction haunted house. Already he'd done a funeral and numerous home and hospital visits, along with a bunch of meetings; he shared some chit-chatty details with Renee as she guided him around, trailed by various teenage crew members. Compared with the just-retired Reverend Clarence, who was seventy-two and going deaf and had been a widower as long as anyone could remember, this one seemed strangely hands-on, but of course he was brand new and concerned with details. Assessing their extension cords; cautioning Renee about dry ice; thumping the plywood walls to make sure they were solid. He squinted at the Volkswagen and warned, "Be sure no one cranks that. Could be deadly if anyone started it indoors." Renee told him she had that under control. (Judging by her expression, this was a lie and the issue had never crossed her mind.) Reverend Jerry gave a small, prim nod. "Good. Fine," he said.

"So that's it," Renee told him, wrapping up the tour. "The kids do a tremendous job with the entire project, and they learn so much responsibility and so many management skills. It's a wonderful learning experience for them." This wasn't Renee's usual way of talking; she sounded like a cop visiting a middle school on Career Day.

Reverend Jerry was still nodding, curious, gazing as if with admiration at their accomplishments; but he didn't look delighted with the entrepreneurial skill-building the youth had undertaken.

"You know, Renee, I'm just not sure the church needs to be in this business," he said. Cathy thought it was, in fact, the *business* aspect of it he was against—the fundraising. She knew about Jesus in the temple, kicking out the greedy moneychangers who were raking in the cash. Maybe he wanted the youth to offer free admission to the haunted house?

As he kept talking, she realized it was the Halloween aspect he minded. Still, however, she managed to misunderstand his objection. She thought he was bothered by the murdery bits, by the thought of the youth play-acting with knives or ropes. That he was like parents with a no-toy-guns policy.

But no. No.

"So we should ask ourselves, do we want church vampires?" That was the wrap-up to his remarks, delivered by the branching corridor that led to the nursery hall. Doors shone. The leaf-brown carpet, moved down here when the sanctuary was remodelled, was still plush. All around were posters, notices, offers, reminders, permission forms for opportunities.

"I'll leave you to think about it," he told the group, and he said his gracious goodbyes and headed off toward the main building. Renee, in her yellow Chestnut Mountain First Baptist polo shirt, one elbow resting on a wide window ledge, thoughtfully studied her group.

"Should we tone down the grue?" a red-haired new kid asked her, and she shook her head.

"I don't know," she said. "I didn't really get what that was about. Look how many years the youth group here has been doing the haunted house, and nobody's ever thought anything but that it was fine. I don't think they would get rid of it now."

Reverend Jerry's objection, it turned out, was to anything eerie. The supernatural, the undead. It wasn't stabbing and strangling that bothered him; it was the idea of the occult.

"But those things aren't real," Cathy told her mom, in the parking lot.

Her mom said, "I think he thinks maybe they are."

"Well, gah," Cathy said. *Gah*, a substitute for taking God's name in vain, was how Christian girls indicated surprise—or one of its opposites, exasperation. It was a word Cathy used often, constantly vacillating, as she did, between amazement and being completely fed up. "It was just old Mr. Bevins under a sheet, Scoob."

The Southern Baptist Convention was at war with itself, the conservative forces battling to drive out the liberals, but in retrospect the numbers seem strangely close. The Convention's conservatives managed sixty percent to forty when they voted in 1981. In 1990, fifty-seven to forty-three. Not ninety to ten, ever.

But a win is a win. The victors dragged the Southern Baptists away from their 1970s tolerance for abortion, away from their senior seminarians' refutation of Adam and Eve as historical figures. The growing interest in universalism—the notion that there was no hell—was killed. Baptists had been fine with nuance and metaphor; that was over. The new crew quashed the idea that Noah's flood hadn't been a single, global event that drowned the earth and spared one family. Books got yanked from shelves; careers were cut short. The task then was to communicate the news, filter it down through all the various levels, start letting the churchgoers know things had changed.

One Saturday afternoon when Cathy arrived for work crew, there was a babble of excited talk. Mitchell, people were saying. Last night. Mitchell and *Renee*.

"What is it?" Cathy asked Mandy. "What's going on?"

"You haven't heard?"

"No." How would she have heard?

"Mitch drove Renee home from the movies—they didn't go together, but I guess they ran into each other there. He wanted her to pray with him, and just talk for a while, is what we heard. But then he—I guess he didn't want to let her out of the car, and he drove her to Knoxville."

"She went to *Knoxville* with him? Last *night*?" She tried to imagine a long car trip with Mitch and that scary beard of his. What on earth would they talk about?

"Well, he sort of took her there," Mandy said. "I mean, kind of against her will. I mean, I guess. He said he loved her."

"Like a—is this like a kidnapping thing?"

"No, no. Well, I don't know. I mean, what's kidnapping? She knows him; she was helping him out and stuff. She just didn't want to go off to wherever with him. Is what I heard."

"That's completely crazy. Was he trying to keep her with him? Did he drive her back home?"

"She took a taxi home, in the middle of the night."

"*What*?" Cathy had never been in a taxi, and the exotic nature of this solution ramped up the strangeness of the story.

"I know. It cost a hundred and sixty dollars, and I guess Reverend Jerry is going to pay for it. I mean, the church, not him personally."

"Did she tell Mitch she loved him back?"

"I don't guess so. I don't think she does. Plus he's way too young for her. A high-schooler? She'd get in big trouble."

This didn't seem to be true, or not in Cathy's experience; the male teachers and coaches and so on who hit on high-school girls never got in big trouble. But, yes, possibly it was different for Renee, and maybe she would get fired. Though Cathy couldn't imagine her wanting to get anything going with Mitchell—one of her charges, and, moreover, one she seemed at most to tolerate with her even-tempered patience.

Cathy said, "Well, is Renee okay? Is she, I don't know, upset or whatever?"

"I don't think so. She didn't seem upset. You know how calm she stays. She was here earlier and she told us a little about it, because everybody knows anyway, and then she went to meet with the deacons and explain. They called a special session to deal with it."

Mitch had to leave—that was the decision. He transferred his membership over to Trinity Baptist, effective immediately, and he took his toolbox with him. The drywall grabbing bar he'd made remained in the crawl space where the team was putting up the Screamers' Tunnel, but no one else had Mitch's deftness with lifting whole walls in one go and effortlessly setting them in place.

Cathy was afraid Renee would be cowed—or, even now, get fired. That didn't happen, though. The next Sunday night at Youth Group, she gave updates not only on the Halloween projects but also on the upcoming dance, Talent Night, and Christmas Family Banquet.

But over the next few days, it felt as if the balance shifted. There was a pattern Cathy would come to recognize over the coming years: a swirl of excitement and gossip around some event that seems to die down quickly but then reappears, like a hurricane spawning smaller storms. Snippets of talk were overheard—in the halls by the restrooms, or in the kitchen during Coffee Hour. Renee's name was mentioned in a wider range of contexts, and not always admiringly. Why had she let

Mitchell get as far as Knoxville? A boy who looked so old. She should know better. Why had she climbed in his car?

It was nothing major; the issue was settled. Except then it wasn't, after all. Renee had been declared not at fault, not to blame. She had, essentially, been doing her job: counselling a youth who needed advice and guidance. But it seemed to Cathy that merely by coming under scrutiny, Renee's credibility was diminished. And suddenly Reverend Jerry was sounding more certain about getting rid of the Haunted House.

The next Saturday the edict came down: no more Halloween. They had six days to transform it into a Harvest Festival. Reverend Jerry volunteered to help them round up hay bales and squash. ("Call me Rev Jer. That's what the kids at my old church said.") There would be Pumpkin Bowling, maybe even dressed-up pets. Also some business called Trunk-or-Treat. Caroline would lead a flower-arranging workshop and help sell popcorn balls. And once again Leon Bass would roll his car into the Annex, this time to be decorated with chrysanthemums, like in the Rose Bowl Parade on television.

All that work.

An upside, though: Cathy did not in fact have to paint with scary Mitchell; instead, she helped Nathan—Clipboard Guy, as she thought of him at first. They drove around in his Vega, returning haunted house props to church members. (Not the candelabra, which they could still use.) Her parents didn't know she was with him; it wasn't a date. But Nathan swung through the Wendy's drive-through for Frosties and fries. And just before the church he pulled over into the Sizzler parking lot and asked her, "Can I have a kiss for my efforts?" Cathy set her fries on the dashboard and leaned toward him and closed her eyes. Her fingers found his hair, and she had never felt anything softer.

Over the years that followed Cathy lost touch with Renee, but never forgot her amused, forgiving wisdom. The way Renee neither hectored nor gave advice.

And she came to think the lasting mystery of that year was how the congregation, and especially the deacons and the search committee, had caught on so early to the atmosphere of control, of pushiness, that was coming down. Matters of doctrine and theology weren't, at that time, discussed much, at least not at the white Baptist churches. Incredible as it would sound later, religion was still generally thought to be private and up to individuals, who were assumed to be guided by common sense. Reverend Clarence, the one lost to retirement, had given a few sermons over the decades on soul liberty—the notion that your relationship with God was your own affair. As a child she'd felt a private kinship with God, that they were a team of two. Back in those pre-Rev Jer days, all the weekly church time, excessive as it seemed, had resulted mainly in resolutions to be kinder, to walk with God, to show more love.

How could they allow that to vanish?

How

Andrea has a juice of some kind, punch, plus little stacks of funeral sandwiches and cookies on a floppy paper plate that promises disaster. Her best friend, Mimi, is clipping along behind her in heels, carrying a refined-looking plate of unproblematic vegetable spears and two sandwich cubes. No messy sweets—more like the choices of a grown woman than of a seventeen-year-old girl. Andrea is in a pale blue Sunday dress, which she worries is not dark enough, and Mimi is wearing a denim skirt and brown plaid blouse. They wend toward the table at one side of the church basement where Andrea's father has claimed three places. He pulls out the chair beside him, courtly, and Andrea sits down; Mimi takes the third seat, murmuring hello toward an elderly, self-contained lady who evidently hears very little. They have not spoken to many people. It's impossible to navigate the throng of well-wishers, so they just signed the book.

Mimi leans across Andrea to say, "Doug, I'm going to get a cup of coffee. Can I bring you one?" He shakes his head, says he's fine. When Andrea first asked him to drive her to the funeral, he said, "I can't sit through all that Catholic hocus-pocus." (In their family, only he talks that way, using "can't" to mean "won't," just as his "I want to" means "I'm going to.") Later he rethought and turned nicer, even though it means Andrea and Mimi are missing a day of school.

The funeral is for the father of Oliver, a boy they babysit. He's dashing lopsidedly around the perimeter of the room, banging into tables, with his aunts after him. Oliver is one of those bruise-covered kids who's always crashing into stuff so that he's never really uninjured. Andrea longs to scoop him up and squeeze him, but he seems not to have noticed her yet. The room is long and noisy, and, though there's no alcohol and of course no festive atmosphere, there's a swell of conversation at a volume that keeps increasing.

Oliver's father, Mr. Hahn, died of a self-inflicted gunshot wound to his head, in a field between the old barn and a new barn he was having built. Three horses were in the pasture near where he died, and Andrea has been wondering if Mr. Hahn went out there to say goodbye to them, to maybe not be alone or to watch something alive and untroubled while he knelt there and made up his mind. It was mucky, spring, and Andrea thought he wouldn't have wanted to lie down in the mud, even though it was about to not matter anymore. Mrs. Hahn was out running errands with Oliver when this happened. She expected him home that evening, but when he didn't return she figured that he'd gone to a hotel.

The delay before he was found seemed to Andrea far from the worst aspect of his death, but nonetheless the loneliest part. "I suppose they'd been fighting a lot, so she thought he wanted some time away from her,"

was the only explanation Andrea's mother could offer
for why he had lain there all night.

In the days before the funeral, Andrea kept picturing
Oliver's little hands, one with his golf ball and the other
clutching his green washcloth. She asked her mother if
they should offer to take him for a few days, and Shelby
said of course; if Andrea wanted to phone, then that
would be a lovely thing to do. She left a message with a
female relative, but Mrs. Hahn didn't get back to her.

And now Mr. Hahn will be buried, here in his dinky
north Georgia hometown, and Mrs. Hahn and Oliver
might move to Asheville or some other place where she
has more family. Though it's too early to say. Oliver zips
around again and Andrea blocks him for the chance to
hold him a moment, Mimi leaning in to nuzzle him too,
until he wriggles away. His hair in fine curls, like the
fragile curves of feathers that show up briefly on the
sleeves of down jackets. Both girls stand there with wet
cheeks, swiping the backs of their hands across their
faces, while Oliver caroms between them with his head
lowered, roaring and growling, being silly like always.

As they prepare to head home, her father asks if
she'd like to rest in the back, and, though Andrea hasn't
stretched out across the seat like that in years, she
wants to now. She falls asleep feeling the tire beneath
her cheek, vibrating up to her through the chassis and
the floor and the foam and the upholstery's velvety nap.
From where she's lying, the road's shiver is equal parts
a sound and a feeling, keeping her company with a reli-
able hum that will not stop, will not even lessen.

An unintended consequence of Mr. Hahn's death is that
it leaves Andrea and Mimi without a summer job. They

were going to split the Oliver-sitting, which would have covered movies and school clothes but also left time for the library and going to the lake. Now they're at a loose end. They are in Andrea's room, lying on her bed with their heads hanging over the side. Andrea is reading, and Mimi is calligraphy-writing MAVIS on her wrist to look like a tattoo.

Mavis is her real name, never used. It was already so outmoded in the mid-Sixties, when the girls were born, that it had no hope of becoming fashionable for another fifty years, and then only in the deliberately nerdy, New Yorkish way of a Hester or an Olive or Edwina. The mismatch between naming the baby Mavis and calling her Mimi was, Andrea has always thought, an indicator of some basic parental disagreement—an inability to settle on how they wanted their child to seem in the world.

Andrea's mother has a different take on it. "To me 'Mimi' is kind of pretentious," Shelby finally admitted. "It's so fancy."

"Foreign, you mean? Too French?"

"Well, rich," her mother said. "Like they're trying to be upper-class."

"Really?" Andrea said, and received an exasperated look. But to her it sounds babied, a name for a poodle with red-painted toenails. She envies Mimi for that indulgent nickname—as if she's always been petted and adored. She hasn't, but even having that aura seems worth something to Andrea.

Now Mimi finishes inking in the S, flops over, and sighs. "We're going to need an income," she says. "What are we going to do?"

"McDonald's?"

Mimi's head goes back and forth on the mattress.

"Someplace at the mall?"

"Outdoors would be better. Wouldn't it?"

"Pool counter?"

"You need lifeguarding to work there," Mimi says.

"Washing cars? Cutting grass? Burger King?" No; no; no. Andrea doesn't suggest babysitting, and neither does Mimi. In fact, they are done with babysitting; neither of them will ever do it again. They do not blame themselves for Mr. Hahn's death—either not at all, or not exactly; and yet it seems possible that some unnoticed indicator flashed past.

"I'll ask my dad," Andrea says. "Maybe he can think of something."

He calls a bunch of cousins, and the next Monday morning they start work at a fruit stand by Coulson's Barbecue. Their training takes about twenty minutes, and their new boss, Drake Coulson, puts a watermelon in the cooler for them and says to cut it when they have a slack time in the afternoon.

"Run over to the restaurant and ask my aunt Beverly for a knife, if you need one," he tells them as he climbs into his pickup. He yells a few last-minute instructions out the truck window, and they're on their own.

"Do you suppose he thought we might have brought our own butcher knives with us?" Andrea asks.

"What kind of job prerequisite is that? Ten-inch knife required!"

It's an auspicious beginning: they're going to have plenty of time to fall over laughing at private jokes and otherwise wasting time. The stand is only busy at lunchtime and in the late afternoon, when people stop for beans and cucumbers on the way home for supper.

The girls start keeping a saucer of cherry tomatoes on the counter, to offer customers with their change—the after-dinner mints of the produce-stand world—because they figure Drake wants them to show entrepreneurial initiative. While things are slow, they trot across the parking lot to refill their cups of ice in the scorching kitchen, where no one seems to mind the slam of the screen door. The cooks and servers call them "doll baby" and "hon" and gave them the last slices of pie to share. Andrea and Mimi don't see this as privilege, but as a confirmation of their nice manners. They never tell their mothers anything, but, if they did mention the pie, it would be to let their moms know they're behaving well, that adults like them.

Drake brings a hammock from his house and sets it up under the oak tree behind the stand, close to the meadow's wire fence.

"It's okay to have a break, as long as you don't keep any customers waiting," he says, and after that they bring stacks of books with them and take turns reading in the hammock, an hour at a time.

The fighting between her parents doesn't seem to have changed, but Andrea's noticing it more.

"Your mom's so dumb," her dad says to Andrea, softly, one night. Her mother is on the phone, sitting on the hall floor and leaning against the wall like a teenager; she's hardly talking, repeating, "Uh-huh. Uh-huh," while she plays with the phone cord. Andrea knows Doug doesn't see her mother's politeness, her patience with this exasperating caller—how willing, or at least prepared, she is to relinquish her evening because someone wants it. What she claims for herself is like an arm-length piece of cloth that keeps getting cut smaller. Sure, the ongoing "uh-huh" is monotonous—annoying, maybe. What's now apparent to Andrea, though, is that he's making a decision to see her mother in a bad light. It's a kind of tax her mother has to try to pay.

Doug's gaze is holding Andrea's, waiting for her to answer. To weigh in on whether her mother is dumb. (Dumb! What a word. She's hardly even heard it since kindergarten.) He is not quite smiling, but a sense of demand—of being pushed, or pulled—is in the air like sound waves. Andrea stares down at her book, at the crease between the pages, wishing she could become tiny and live in there. She bends back the halves of the book, cracking the spine. Turns a few chapters, cracks it again. Her father's stare lessens its intensity, as if he's not trying anymore to trap her into agreement.

"I don't know," she whispers, and gets up. "I'm going to check on Stacy." She will have to pay for the library book.

Upstairs, her younger sister is lying on their parents' bed, chin on her stacked fists, staring at a Tide commercial. Their mother's half of her phone call floats up the stairwell in brief, separate replies: "Yes."

"I see."

"Uh-huh."

Their mom does office work at a dental practice and is taking classes to become a radiology technician. She isn't dumb. Andrea can only fix on that thought clearly, though, now that she's in another room.

She asks Stacy, "Whatcha watching?"

"*Three's Company* rerun," she says.

"You're not supposed to watch that. They think you're not old enough," Andrea says, and lies down on the empty space on the bed. "Which one is this?"

The sisters lie there, side by side, watching bird-brained Chrissy argue with Jack and Janet, while the goatish Mr. Roper pretends to tinkle a little bell to mock Jack's supposed gayness. They have seen this one before. Their dad's footsteps start up the stairs.

"Turn it off," Andrea says. "He'll get mad." Stacy doesn't answer.

He pokes his head in the doorway, sees a girl pouting on the screen. "Turn off that garbage," he says. Stacy doesn't budge, but Andrea slides her legs toward the floor.

He says, "Stacy, move it. Go get ready for bed."

Downstairs, their mother replaces the receiver, but she doesn't come upstairs. "Somebody's in a snit," Doug says.

Mrs. Hahn has invited Andrea to come say goodbye to Oliver. When they're driving back home afterwards, Andrea's mother stops at Dairy Queen without even asking. She parks where they always do, looking down over a mini playground. At the monkey bars, two children seem to be trying to hang from the dangling legs of their older siblings, who just want to swing across unaccosted. Andrea and Shelby watch, taking careful bites of chocolate shellwork.

"He'll forget me," Andrea says. Oliver's little sneakers. His earnest explanations about Nilla Wafers or buckles or his orange crocodile.

Shelby doesn't answer immediately. She eats a chocolate shard, considers. "He probably will," she says.

"Soon? Right away?"

"I don't think so," her mother says. "I expect once they're in a new house, somewhere else, he won't have many opportunities to think about you. But he'll remember you if someone mentions you to him."

"His mother won't talk about me, will she? Me and Mimi?"

"I don't know her that well, baby, but I wouldn't think so. I imagine she'll want to put all this behind her."

Andrea nods. The back of Shelby's head is blonde and grey, tawny stripes with crunchy-looking hairsprayed waves at the bottom. "Does it make you really sad?" Andrea wants to know.

"It's complicated for me," her mother says. She pokes at the dashboard with a key. "After he died, of course I was shocked and horrified. Heartbroken for Oliver, and wondering how Eileen was going to manage. But also, I felt relieved." Jab. Jab. "And that upset me."

"Relieved, why?"

"I won't run into him around town. I won't bump into him. And I haven't found any way to be sorry about that part."

"Why didn't you want to see Mr. Hahn?"

The younger monkey-bar siblings get the bigger ones dragged down, and thin cries of victory float above the parking lot. Mr. Hahn is somewhat attractive, maybe, for an old middle-aged guy. The last piece of cone won't go down. She remembers her dad's complaining about her mother's coldness.

"Your father borrowed money from him," her mother says.

Andrea's breath is just an intake and a cottony dread.

"Had he paid him back?"

Her mother shakes her head. "I'd always feel very, very . . . ashamed, every time I saw Arthur. So realizing that I wouldn't run into him anymore—that was a relief to me."

"Why would Dad think he could? Could do that?"

"Your dad has poor judgment," her mom says.

So. Suicide can solve more than one person's problems. And the person who dies isn't the only one who may gain some form of rest.

Over the next few days she works up the courage to ask for more details. This is an effort to make it less awful, but the answers give her little to work with. (No, not just like forty dollars. "How much?" "I'm not going to tell you." No, Mr. Hahn wasn't the only one. "Who else?" "I'm not going to tell you." Such protectiveness is of limited usefulness at this point, Andrea feels.)

Mimi's around, so there's less time to worry—she's like family, but the kind of family that keeps you from going to pieces. Late July is so oppressive, they set up a messy nest of blankets and sleeping bags on the screen porch and start camping out there, falling asleep on their pile and crawling under the top layers as the night air cools around them. Until they drift off, they play Crazy Eights by flashlight, saving up jacks to use against each other. Andrea's parents occupy the lighted rooms; from the shadowy porch, the living room looks like an aquarium, with talk so soundless, the words vanish as they're said.

One night her father comes out to check on them. He's been turning out lights, locking up. He's in his t-shirt and shorts. Not his regular shorts—his briefs. Andrea's volcanic fear is immediate and multipart; she's rendered mute. He sits down on the arm of one of the porch chairs and updates the girls on the program he was just watching. His feet are pale in a rectangle of lamplight from the living room, and the rest of him can barely be seen. She glances at his shorts. She knows they're made of shirt-like material, or a little thinner. Only two impulses come into her mind—smother; run.

Mimi is still giggling, with an unbothered air that calms Andrea down a bit, lets her think, *Okay, I'm overreacting*.

"Can Poley sleep out here with us?" Mimi asks him. Poley, their dachshund, sleeps at the foot of Stacy's bed, but with treats can be bribed into infidelity.

Doug shakes his head. "Poley wouldn't be happy out here with just you two for company," he says. "Good night, girls. Don't stay up talking too late." He closes the sliding door and moves away.

Andrea is wondering what to say: "That was weird"? "My dad's so rude"? But Mimi seems not to have minded or even noticed anything.

"Your dad's funny," she says. They play another couple of hands of cards. Staying up feels like a strategy to put off having to wake up in the morning.

One mid-August Friday when Mimi gets to the fruit stand, she says she can't work that afternoon. "I've got to get some stuff for school," she says.

"Don't you want to do that together?" Andrea asks.

"It's not clothes or anything," Mimi says. "Just a bunch of little things I need to take care of."

"Well, okay," Andrea says. "I'll man the station." She pops a warm cherry tomato in her mouth and bites down. Some days the girls eat a quart of them for lunch.

But around one-thirty, it's not either of Mimi's parents who pulls up. It's Doug. Andrea thinks he's come for her, that something is wrong. A death; a gunshot. He keeps the engine running and waves to the girls in their tall windowed box.

"One sec!" Mimi calls.

"What is it?" Andrea asks. "What's going on?"

"I asked your dad if he had time to help me with my errands, and he said he could, if we went today."

"You can't go somewhere with my dad."

"Hey, relax. I wanted him to help me out. We're going to K-mart and the drugstore. I won't even be that long." She's off her metal stool and through the empty doorway, leaving Andrea at the counter with the cash drawer and two peck baskets of zucchini, feeling foolish.

Mimi's back in time to close up the stand, carrying four plastic bags.

"See? It was fine," she says. "I got everything done."

Andrea thinks of cats—how they have a precision she needs now, an ability to place each footfall just where they want it. For them it's effortless. "Where'd you come from? Where's my dad?"

"He went in the restaurant to order dinner. He's parked over there. I guess you guys are having barbecue."

"Aren't you coming over?" Andrea says. They don't have a real plan, but most weekends this summer Mimi has been at Andrea's. Now she shakes her head.

"Nah, can't tonight," she says. "We're going to my grandma's. It's her birthday." Mimi looks as if a smile is being held inside her mouth, like a SweeTart.

"So you went to K-mart and shopped. That was your date?" Andrea manages the word lightly.

Mimi looks back at her, choosing among various answers. "What makes something a date?" she finally asks.

On the following days Andrea can't tell if she and Mimi have put that topic behind them or are edging up to it. She starts to have a feeling that cars are bearing down on her. She pictures a big sedan, a Caprice or Impala, barrelling into the stand and killing them both. The best place to escape this persistent image is in the hammock, underneath the oak with its fifty-foot-wide canopy. In the dog days she can't tackle new books anymore and sticks to titles she's read to death, opening a book at random and reading a few paragraphs at a time. A few words, sometimes, before the book slips shut.

The last week of summer, they vow to eat nothing other than stand stuff. From the start, Drake has told them to help themselves, but now the harvest pace has accelerated, and he's urging more on them. "I hate it to go to waste," he says. "Eat it up."

The girls have lost weight on their diet of constant produce-grazing—an unanticipated benefit. "Look how loose these are getting," Mimi says, tugging at her shorts. She slips her hand down the front of the waistband and pulls it forward, showing Andrea the shadowy gap. "The watermelon-and-raw-beans-and-corn diet." They love Drake's Silver Queen corn and keep toothpicks from the restaurant under the counter. When a car pulls into the lot, they do a surreptitious lightning-fast cleaning.

"Me, too," Andrea says, hitching her shorts up. "These are falling off me."

"This has been a good gig," Mimi says. "You think Drake will hire us again next summer?"

"We've been stellar workers, haven't we?"

"Think so," says Mimi doubtfully. How can they know?

They've never been employees before, not really; have never been promoted or fired or interviewed. Have never seen better opportunities and resolved to move on. They wouldn't even know how to quit.

"What do you want to do?" Andrea asks.

"What, tonight? This weekend?"

"No, with your life. Your career."

"Oh, *do*!" Mimi says. "Do! Be!"

"Yeah, *be*," Andrea says.

"God, Andie; I don't know yet," Mimi says. "Your stepmother?"

"Not funny," Andrea says.

"Sure it is," Mimi says. "Don't get in a snit. I don't know. A teacher, maybe. Something with art. Or drama. You?"

"Real estate," Andrea says, an answer that pops out of nowhere and means nothing.

That fall and winter they will grow apart, and in the spring they don't talk about working together. Mimi no longer comes over on weekends. She gets hired in the shoe department at Belk's; Andrea's at the paddle-boat counter at the lake. What she remembers best from the previous summer is the tree canopy. Not just green, but so wide, spreading above the fruit stand and the parking lot and nearly over to the restaurant. She remembers lying there as if protected, gazing up at the oak and the sky, hearing the screen door and the meadow sounds and the loving rustle of hundreds of thousands of separate leaves.

Near Hickory

The boys were six but still napped sometimes on hot, airless days, and then I was allowed to go up to my room and read through the stack of Agatha Christie paperbacks on the upstairs landing. Back then I nurtured a protective and admiring tenderness for Poirot, not yet having concluded he was an ass with a world-class ego. I was up to *Cat Among the Pigeons* one afternoon when the phone rang three times in fifteen minutes. I wandered downstairs to find out if something was going on that I should assist with. Judy—Mrs. Bennett, though she'd told me to use her first name, so I was stuck saying "Judy" but "Mr. Bennett," which seemed to me mismatched and also sexist—was replacing the receiver at the sunroom desk. She looked fraught.

"Casey, Mr. Bennett's father has had a serious stroke," she told me. "In Memphis. The whole family will be flying there, probably tomorrow afternoon." She was jotting on her notepad.

Well. "I'm so sorry," I said. My voice sounded artificial, but I didn't know what to add. Was I part of the whole family? I didn't know whether I'd be expected to go along to take care of the boys, or to stay behind in Glenbrae. Memphis wasn't that many hours away; no one I knew would think of flying there rather than driving. I assumed I'd be part of a drive, but tickets changed the equation.

Judy focused on me for a moment. "I don't know what we'll do about you," she said, not unkindly. "We'll have to work it out. Don't let me forget."

Well, no.

I was the au pair—a title I associated with Bain de Soleil ads, not plain old American college students working for the summer in the North Carolina mountains. "Au pair" did sound splendid, though. The boys were wild but sweet: shy Cameron, with his throaty, endearing chuckle, and lovely Rush, with his plump carrot-shaped fingers and a tangle of pale ringlets that I'd try to coax smooth when he buried his face against me. Their backyard was large enough for us to turn croquet into a dangerous sort of lacrosse with mallets. By the end of my first week, the lethally heavy, hardwood croquet balls were missing most of their paint. Nobody seemed to mind; everything in the three-storey vacation house was old and solid and had been sitting in the same place for decades. As long as nothing actually went missing, no one was likely to notice whether Cameron and Rush and I had damaged anything, since maybe Great-Uncle Mac had dinged it up back in 1904.

Tighe, Mr. Bennett's daughter from his first marriage, flew home that evening for the next day's flight to Memphis. All this flying. She was two years older than I was and attended the University of Michigan, where she would be a senior in the fall. We were to share my room; she usually slept in the basement bedroom when she came to the summer house, but this summer it had been turned into a train room for the boys. All the rooms had names and purposes: workroom, morning room, Judy's office, art room (with its long porcelain sink and intimidating, professional-looking easels, and generations' worth of abandoned paintings). There were plenty of places for Tighe to sleep besides my room, but it was true there was none that went by the name "bedroom." Or perhaps she just wanted someone nearby who'd feel compelled to listen to her.

I was worried about dealing with Tighe, but she was friendly and liked to talk. She sat on the velvet-padded window seat of the room we were going to share that night, which already felt less mine than hers, and unpacked an adult-looking carry-on that held many little pouches and cases. The Bennetts and their friends, I'd observed, liked containers inside other containers. She unzipped a plaid leather bag, took out a handful of eyeliner pencils, and began sharpening them over the wastebasket next to the dresser. She was keyed up and exuberant, the grandfather's illness notwithstanding, because apparently things were great with her boyfriend. His name (archaically, I thought) was Wallace. He swam at Michigan. He was a history major. He was thinking of trying out for a part in a comic one-act play about road rage. He had a single room, and Tighe had a roommate, so they spent most of their time at his dorm. Sometimes they read aloud to each other; they had recently finished a memoir by M.F.K. Fisher, a name I didn't know. Wallace was an accomplished cook; he'd been into beef lately, so Tighe found she was eating more meat. He usually made braises and stir-fries, but when they went out, he liked to try different cuts of steak at all kinds of restaurants.

I had never heard of someone sampling steaks like that, the way you might try out the cookies at different bakeries around town, and I watched her as she shook out her wavy hair and tousled it with her fingers and filled in details about his eating habits. She had blue eyes and very dark curls. Tighe was pretty—much more so, I thought, than I was—though afterwards I wondered how much of this came from her vivacity and confidence. She couldn't stop talking, and all she talked about was Wallace. I pictured them going out a couple of times a week to highly regarded steak places in—where did she go to school, anyway; Bloomington? Tighe would be in a silky tank top printed with roses, a light trench coat tossed over her arm. In my mind they were on a busy street in the lucky, noisy student town, with old-fashioned lamp-posts under a black sky; like a Thomas Kinkade paint-ing but sexy. Though I couldn't picture Wallace's face, Tighe was clear to me, putting up her hand at a corner to summon a taxi, telling the driver in sure tones which restaurant they were trying out that night.

I didn't even know the vocabulary to talk about that interest of theirs. Prime rib, strip loin, porterhouse, T-bone, ribeye; it would be gibberish. I wanted to ask her if she didn't think it was an odd thing to pursue. How old was this Wallace, anyway? He sounded like a dad. In a few years he'd be one of those people who discussed brandy. Scotch; he was probably into that already.

The guys I dated drank Rolling Rock beer and made BLTs or their famous chili. When we went out to eat, it was usually at some place that served all-day breakfast, which was what everyone at the table ordered. We did not dress up or consider our clothes much before we went out. My life seemed to me simpler and more amateurish than Tighe's, with fewer considerations and mental lists. I couldn't imagine I would change enough in two years to become like her (I didn't think I'd ever be like her; she was nearly another species). But it struck me that it wasn't just her family's money that made us different.

Now I would call it privilege: the myriad, tiny rivulets of entitlement that course down through every aspect of someone's days. At the time, though, I was unaware of the concept of privilege. I saw it but could not name it. What separated me from Tighe was, I thought, her massive confidence. Listening to her, I realized how small and constrained my sphere of operation was, and that there were ways of smiling and confronting the world that I would never be ready for.

Moreover, she seemed to have a tighter bond with Wallace than I'd ever had with a boyfriend; he was edging toward husband duties. He *shopped* with her, in *home* stores, for *wedding* presents—incremental layers of intimacy that I found bizarre and unknowable.

"We love all the same things," she told me. "The other day we were shopping for a friend of ours who's getting married. We were looking at the things they were registered for at Macy's, and we were just perfectly in synch. It was like, *No, that's ugly. This is classic. This is what I'd choose.*"

"Wow," I said feebly. "Was this after one of your steak dinners?"

Tighe laughed. "Yes!" she said. "We'd been to this bistro Wallace had been wanting to try, called the Salt

Cellar. I had the New York strip. It was great. And then I remembered we needed to get this gift."

"Did the people in the store think you two were the ones getting married?" I asked.

She laughed again, giddy over the memory. "The clerk did! You are psychic, Casey. She asked us if we were registering, if we were looking at china patterns, all of that. We told her no, but it was really fun. We walked around the store holding hands, just talking about what we would choose. We were *totally* in synch. I loved it."

My childhood best friend Pam and I had done much the same thing when we were young, paging through the Sears catalog. I hadn't thought it meant anything.

By the time we went to sleep, I'd heard enough about Wallace to form strong opinions, in the one-sided way often made possible by the content of girls' conversation. Wallace would never know I existed, yet I knew about his little sister's ferret and his dad's cancer scare.

I'd have liked to hear about Tighe's friends who were actually getting married, although marriage baffled and horrified me. Tattoos were just coming into vogue for the mainstream, and I had the same feeling about them: You understand this is forever, right? Though the age difference between me and Tighe was small, none of my friends were married or engaged or even, as far as I knew, thinking of such a step. Surely it was the permanence that carried the risk, and maybe that risk was part of the attraction; but it seemed unthinkably foreign to me.

"I can't imagine getting married," I said. "I mean, sure, in a way. I've been in love. But wedding vows—no."

She laughed. "Really? You can't see it?" As if this were a lapse of imagination on my part, rather than its opposite.

I was almost sorry for her, about this one small piece of her life; not that she needed my sympathy. How could I find her way of thinking somehow pitiable and yet still feel so clumsy around her? *Young* was the closest I came to identifying how I felt, but I knew it wasn't quite accurate. *Unseasoned*, maybe. There was no way to tell her, "I probably seem prim and babyish to you." I had seen people try to address someone else's misconceptions; my experience was that conversations that began, "You probably think I. . . ." never went well. I left the issue unaddressed; Tighe was too preoccupied, anyway, to notice. She made an effort, though. As I say, she was nice.

"Where are you from?" she asked me.

"Conover," I said. She looked questioning. "It's near Hickory," I added.

"Oh, okay," she said. I was irked with her for not knowing where it was—did she feel free to be completely oblivious? It didn't occur to me that I only knew most of North Carolina's towns now because I went to UNC and met people from all over the state. If you had always lived in the same place and then gone to college out of state, you wouldn't necessarily learn all these little map dots. I felt as if both I and my small hometown, with its failure to register as significant, were being judged. Next to her fireball energy, I was like part of a person.

The grandfather died during the night. The phone calls started about five a.m.

When Mr. Bennett and Judy started figuring out the logistics, I saw that I was in the way. Their concern for me was real but abstract—I was very much a second- or third-tier problem for them then. This meant that, even though I was their responsibility for the summer, I'd become a pesky logistical challenge.

"Can you go back to Chapel Hill?" Judy asked. I was miserable, miserable.

"I'm moving to a different dorm this fall," I said. "It's rented out for summer students, and so is the dorm I had this year."

I didn't have a car, and my parents and brother were in New Orleans on vacation, and there wasn't an easy way to get me home to Conover. The neighbours they were close to weren't at their mountain houses just then, so there was no one to hand me over to. I was young enough that I still only travelled with my parents, and they mostly took me when they went somewhere; it wouldn't occur to them to do anything else.

In the end, I was to stay in the house by myself for a couple of days. Mr. Bennett would fly back to North Carolina right after the funeral to tie up some work projects, drive me wherever I was going to go—home to Conover, I supposed—and then head back to Tennessee to, presumably, start settling the estate.

Because there would be no saying goodbye to the grandfather, the Bennetts took an extra day to prepare. Their lives, though, were so complex, they were still slapping together hasty arrangements as they loaded the boys in the Volvo to head out. Cameron and Rush and I hugged hard, and made silly faces through the car windows. I'm sure all three of us thought we would see one another again.

"Casey, just help yourself. Cook whatever you want, and there's that lasagna in the fridge. Finish off the pear juice." Judy told me. "Call us at Jack's sister's house if there's an emergency; the number's on the desk."

"Okay, thank you. I will. Take good care. I'm sorry this happened," I said. I was, too; but I was also at an age of conflicting desires and intentions, and feeling bad for them hadn't kept me from resolving to go through their whole house, top to bottom, to see what I could learn. I decided this while they discussed whether to send me back to Chapel Hill with a cousin of the club's tennis pro, or whether Mr. Bennett's ex-wife might be able to do something. She'd phoned a couple of times, willing to help (Tighe liked everyone to get along, and I guess they tried), but Judy didn't want to take her up on it.

Now the discomfort caused by my burdensome-ness overrode my liking of and loyalty to the boys. I was affronted that Judy hadn't been more concerned about me. I felt no compunction toward Mr. Bennett, only wariness, so I didn't care what he would think of my investigating his home, as long as he didn't catch me. Looking at their things was a small, educational crime, and it was one I felt entitled to commit.

I had never spent a night alone in a house in my life. I decided to stay awake reading all night, with a fire-place poker by the bed, prepared for anything. My book was *The Godfather*—long and engrossing enough to keep me awake until morning. Around three, though, I put it down. There was a hot spell that week. Glen-brae houses had not been built with air conditioning and almost never needed it; escaping the heat was the reason people went to the mountains in the first place. Night flowed in through my open window.

What I felt coming into the room was not just the breeze on my legs and the pine scent, which was the essence of summer, but also an unfamiliar sense of aloneness. Who knew where I was? Small in a house, one lamp, dark yard, trees everywhere, night at every window and over me. This was a new kind of privacy, so large and complete, and lasting so long.

The next day, after I woke up alive and hefted the poker and checked the deadbolts and ate my toast, I thought about my exploring campaign. What if they had some kind of fancy remote recording device? This was before nanny cams, years before the internet. But I worried, half ridiculously, half with reason, that they might have some system in place for intruders that would trap me. Winter break-and-enter problems. Still, how humiliating if I got snared in such a mess. Thinking this slowed but did not deter me. I had one chance to learn more about their lives, and it seemed to me I'd regret it if I missed it.

So I opened drawers, looked in the nightstands, held bottles up to the light. Nothing was revelatory; things held only the intrinsic interest of being not my own. I was curious about utility bills, care labels (everything was pure—100 percent cotton, or silk, or cashmere), the paraphernalia of wealth and adulthood.

At the attic doorway, I hesitated, then went up the stairs, fearful but determined. At the top of the narrow staircase, bare wood and echoey, I looked at the suitcases, an old sewing machine, boxes labelled "books," in Judy's script. There was a storage room on one side of the attic. I was afraid to open the door, though there was no lock on it. What if Mr. Bennett or Judy had rigged it to explode outward in a chaotic burst of stuff I could never gather up again? What if it turned out to be a gun cupboard? It took me five minutes to turn the handle, even after I knew I was going to do it.

Inside were benches. They were turned up on end, six of them, with black leather seats. Nearly everything decorative in the house had been new to me that summer: Toby jugs; Staffordshire; Lladro. But to my surprise, I recognized these. They were Barcelona. I didn't know Mies van der Rohe; but I had seen one of his benches in the foyer of the Mint Museum in Charlotte on a visit with my grandmother and been so taken with it that I asked the desk attendant if it was something special. She told me the name, and that it was a famous furniture design from the Thirties.

I said, "It's beautiful."

"Yes. The proportions are perfect," she said.

"Can you buy them?" I asked. "I mean, just anyone, not a museum?"

"Oh, yes. They're sold by a company called Knoll. Here, I'll write it down for you. It's great that you like it! I have to tell you, though, they're pricey. Four thousand dollars. You can write to the company for a brochure, if you wish."

I had felt my heart go out to the Barcelona bench, there in the museum, the way girls in adolescence often develop instant and lasting loyalties that never really leave them afterwards. Proportion, she had told me; and it was true—that bench had a perfection of proportion that had brought me to a standstill. Now here I was on the threshold of the Bennetts' attic storage space, gazing at six of them, carefully stacked side by side. The floor of the large storage room had been spread with sheets under the benches, and white sheets were also draped to protect them from dust. Hang tags on a leg of each bench said "spring" and "fall" with up and down arrows; these, I realized after studying them, were instructions for turning the benches while they were being stored. I figured Mr. Bennett was going to put them in his law office; I'd seen a photo of him at the office, and it was modern, all black and silver.

Had the Bennets inherited the Barcelonas? Won them in a poker game? Bought them cheap from someone who went bankrupt? Whatever their provenance, this was the first time I saw how rich people hoard money until they pass it along to other rich people.

And of course I was pleased, proud, even, that I recognized them. In those years I was very focused on credit, fairness, acknowledgment being given where it was due. It felt as if considerable credit was due to me, for spotting the bench in the museum and understanding how finely made, how well designed, it was. I had responded to it as if I were answering a call; I had good instincts. This meant a lot, surely? Or did it merely mean the design was great? Was it me, or Mies van der Rohe? (That Ed Bennett should also get some credit for knowing good design was a notion I failed to entertain, believing, as I did then, that everything was handed to him whole and intact.)

And the money; there was no getting around that. This was twenty-four thousand dollars' worth of furniture, stored in an attic closet. It was a good chunk of what my parents had paid for our house, when they bought it when I was three.

A few years later, I had finished my B.A. and was half killing time, half thinking about graduate school in journalism. I was still living in Chapel Hill, but it had changed for me. It was, of course, as refined a place as Bloomington (or Ann Arbor).

I met someone who had known the Bennetts. Paula and I were waiting tables for the summer at an upscale casual place on Franklin Street, one of those *Southern Living*-famous restaurants. We talked while we rolled the flatware in napkins nice enough to wear as scarves and stacked them in woven baskets.

She remembered Rush and Cameron, but not with the fondness I retained for them. Her Glenbrae summer had been the year before mine. She had worked in the pro shop at their country club, she told me, and done occasional babysitting for those families in the evenings, after the golf games had wound down. When the Bennetts had guests over who also had small kids, they liked to have another sitter there to support the au pair and keep everything running smoothly.

"The first time I went, they told me that, because they had a live-in sitter and just needed someone to help her out, they only paid two dollars an hour. And I did it anyway," she said. Her voice was tight. "And then I helped them again, a couple of weeks later. I was afraid I'd get in trouble with my job if I turned them down. And that second night, their sitter wasn't there; she was away for the weekend, on her break. And still, when I left after four hours, they gave me eight dollars." She shook her head. "Minimum wage was three thirty-five.

I was counting quarters then. But I didn't know how to turn them down, and they could tell."

I said, "That's . . . that's wage theft."

"I know," she said.

I wondered whether it was Judy or Mr. Bennett who handed Paula her eight dollars, not even just giving her a ten-dollar bill. Paula herself couldn't remember. Both seem possible, barely. (I mean, they were nice. But still.)

I hardly knew them, those few weeks I was living with them. It was when Reagan had faced off with the air traffic controllers' union and started his rise to god-like status on the right. Now I think maybe the Bennetts took a purposeful satisfaction in underpaying. I'd heard them grouse about their taxes. Who was there to tell them that their math was off; that more workers on a job don't mean the same amount of wages, divided into smaller piles?

They could not have done it by accident, or without thinking. I can see myself, if I'd been Paula, wanting to believe they had merely forgotten, on that one evening, that their au pair was away. Maybe they imagined babysitters had extra money lying around, money they just didn't need. They had been fair with me—which, I guess, means only that they felt like it.

At first I couldn't picture Judy counting out a five and three ones; and then I could. I hadn't known, growing up, that some people can meet your eyes and still cheat you.

That day I saw and immediately fell for the Barcelona bench, on a museum trip when I was seventeen, I promised myself, the way you do, "Someday I'll have one of these."

I don't have one, or want one anymore. But, yes, their proportions are perfect. Perfect.

I was not sophisticated, as a girl. I couldn't say the things I needed to. But my instincts, which have served me so well, were sound. My memory of that night alone is of my sudden, vast privacy; the dark pines; how the air turned cold by the middle of the night. My bedside lamp at the window, as small, from the outside, as one flame. I knew it would not always be this way. Fates were converging. A car would pull up, sometime in my future. I would climb in. We would drive away. The satiny night would move like silent water. No one would hear us; no one would know where we were. Everything I wanted would unfold.

Midway

I was procrastinating at work, trying to figure out what's happening in Togo, when Maura entered the lunch-room with the look she gets when she's had another dream that I died. It's this elevated, pitying expression; she examines me as if I were a double exposure—my coming ghost superimposed over my just-barely-hanging on, corporeal form, like I'm already draining out. It happens about once a quarter, even though I've told her there's no need to keep me updated.

There's always fruitcake on a counter in the lunch-room. All of us have long since eaten a lifetime's sup-ply, but cutting off a sliver in an intentional way is useful for changing the topic. You can say, Do you think these pecans are maybe not quite as good as last year's, then discuss which supplier they're from; or just chew thoughtfully and gesture toward your cheek when some-one speaks, indicating that your thoughts are occupied with quality control. Being able to switch subjects on the fly is necessary when you work for an outfit that employs so many family members and therefore delivers all sorts of unnecessary conflict into your life. Maura's my cousin Glenn's third wife, and I wish they would hurry up and get divorced so she would feel moved to quit here and go bother people somewhere else with her witchy predictive visions.

"Tracy, I had the dream again," Maura said today, in a half-whisper clearly intended to convey some useful information or actionable warning; but really, what am I meant to do?

"The dream," I said. "Um, would you be willing to stop telling me about it? Because I never know how to react."

"Well, personally, I aim to live in a state of readiness," Maura said.

"I see," I said. Once again I wished we were large enough, and non-family enough, to have an actual HR department that would tackle this for me. (That's one of those things that's always seemed to me like an indicator of success: you're supported by HR professionals who offer sound advice and make your life better. That, and wearing heels to work.) "I don't live in a state of readiness, precisely, Maura, and I don't see that changing soon. It would mean a lot to me if you could just not tell me when you dream about attending my visitation hours at Dwyer Funeral Home, or whatever. Can you see that?"

"Of course, absolutely. It's just that, you know, I'm guided by my intuition. That's what I listen to. I'm sorry if it makes you uncomfortable."

I said, "Well, if you could just try." I shaved off a sliver of Southern Traditional and held it out. The jewel-like candied fruit gleamed—the most easily mocked ingredient, but also the best. Fruitcake is not well understood. When you study those little shining cubes, you can see faint ridges left by the paring knife's serrations, and if you concentrate, you can sometimes feel them on your tongue. I asked her, "What do you think of the pecans in this? A little lacking?"

Our fruitcakes are sold with two different wrappings. One line uses the silver and bright green label my aunt Phyllis designed in twenty minutes, forty years ago, with the same swirly logo as always; you can even see a jog in her handwriting on the K in Peskin's. The other looks like one from an entirely separate company, with an understated label in white, cream, and pale gold, and a refined, crisp font. It has a star that's just long lines, like in Christmas art with the shepherds closing in on the stable. Our dated packaging is favoured by the older crowd, while the newer iterations are bringing in a more sophisticated, younger buyer. It's amazing how much a clean typeface and a cotton tag with a rose-gold grommet can accomplish.

My cousin Kat runs the marketing department, which is her and Gail, our old babysitter. Gail handles CRM and, in the off season, graphic design. She's finishing her master's at Georgia State—very slowly, because she's a single mom and is basically eternally frazzled. It works out fine, though, because it lets the two of them mull over strategic decisions and implement one small but meaningful change at a time. We tend to innovate gradually here.

Often with a situation like Togo, I sort of have a handle on what's happening, but I can't get the traction that would make it interesting. In so many other areas, knowing the bare minimum doesn't make the topic opaque and boring. I can recall numerous times a single sentence transformed my understanding of something in biology, or history, or various Hollywood gossip stories. With politics, though, it's just a bunch of random names if you don't grasp the issues.

So I slogged through some coverage about president Faure Gnassingbé; background on his father, Gnassingbé Eyadéma; and opposition leaders Jean-Pierre Fabre (National Alliance for Change) and Tikpi Atchadam (Panafrican National Party). But it's not as if I knew, after reading, where I'd throw my support, if I were voting there. And I'd gained only the sketchiest idea about any issues beyond the ruling party's decades-long stranglehold on power.

The only way I can see to learn even a tiny bit of this stuff—aside from getting an online subscription to *République Togolaise* (and even so, I wouldn't know whether I was reading their equivalent of the *Telegraph*, the *Times*, the *Guardian*, or the *Independent*)—would be reading every *Economist* cover to cover. But in my experience, any magazine that comes weekly is one that's always showing up before you've really wrapped up the previous issue; plus the thought of all those extra stories, on wordy, impenetrable subjects that are way beyond me, just preemptively wears me out.

Moreover, once I figure out Togo even a little, there's the faint hope of getting up to speed on Cameroon, with its impassioned, ongoing demonstrations for Paul Biya to step down. And in Zimbabwe Robert Mugabe finally left, but it was a positive outcome achieved very questionably, through a soft coup. The challenge for me, always, lies in sorting the scant facts I encounter and trying to make sense of them before I forget it all. Ellen Johnson Sirleaf: yes or no? (I feel like George Bush, the second one: *So who are the good guys,* he's said to have asked an advisor.) How's Nigeria doing since Muhammadu Buhari's re-election, and what did Goodluck Jonathan do after stepping down from the presidency?

And that's just the barest skeleton of news developments in a handful of sub-Saharan African countries; ideally I'll brush up on Australia (are they Conservative now, or Labour again? Wasn't that Julia someone, the last prime minister I remember, already a couple of elections ago?); also New Zealand; where's Scotland these days with the Brexit discord; plus the Irish border issue, has Narendra Modi made much progress on getting every Indian household a new toilet, why is Abbas's standing so low among his electorate, is Sara Netanyahu going to actually discuss the shady bottle-recycling grift, why has Abe suddenly gained popularity in Japan, I thought everybody hated him. And, and. Mining CEO Don Blankenship is out of prison (how much time did he actually serve? a few weeks?) and itching to get into politics; stay alert, West Virginia. Also those Volkswagen executives who defrauded the world with their emissions scam—only a couple received jail sentences, which seems to me like an issue some German voters might want to raise a fuss about.

And I have no idea what's up in Uruguay, Portugal, Zambia, Sri Lanka, Slovenia. I'm behind on everything, all the time. A few years ago Belgium was flying apart, *was about to cease to exist*; but apparently they avoided that outcome and are still functioning. Not that I'd necessarily know if the country had vanished.

I said, "See you," to Maura and headed to my office, warming my hands with my Nespresso in the red-rimmed mug I favour. People half-wash the mugs but don't scrub them, because everyone's family here. (The bakery side is held to higher standards, obviously.) When you drink milk or water, you can still taste the last person's coffee. I'm sure it's an illusion that I can tell who used a cup last—I know everyone who works here very well indeed, but not enough to identify their imagined spit. I settled at my desk, comfortable in the knowledge that no one was really going to object if I frittered the afternoon away reading news stories. We're not busy now, and I'm part of my family like a fork in a stack of same-sized forks, resting in the drawer. They're not going to give up on me.

For Christmas when I was little, we always went over to Payday and Pip Pip's (Payday was what we called my great-grandmother, for long-forgotten reasons); they cooked two turkeys and a ham, and opening presents took all day. Payday and her sisters and the aunts, Phyllis and Bev and Simone and the whole crew, seemed to spend all fall wrapping. They tended to start off strong but finish by just slapping some scraps of paper around the package. The gift pile was a sort of escarpment that ran along the back wall of Payday and Pip Pip's living room. It was banked up three feet high in places and sloped downward across half the carpet, an avalanche gradually encompassing the living room floor. There must have been a thousand presents there—thirty or more people all giving stuff to one another. I envied families who opened gifts one at a time, everyone gazing on and attentive to each separate unveiling.

Pip Pip and Payday weren't rich, though that insane cascade of gifts made it look like they had all the money in the world. (Every year a few fragile things turned up crushed under the weight of the accrual, but there were too many other presents for anyone to get over-excited about some minor losses.) That was before our fruitcakes took off around the South; it was much more a small-time regional offering then. There was none of the logistics expertise we have now, or the supply chain management, or the testing. We didn't have Holiday Scones or Cider Punch Clusters. It was just Uncle Foster driving vanloads of product up to Tennessee or over to Alabama on weekends, and Uncle Jason and Aunt Kathleen running the fall evening shift until Julie was born and they had to slow down for a while. So far even the older generations are not wealthy, partly because all this payroll means we're kind of like the Saudi ruling family absorbing all the oil royalties; but back then they were definitely not rich. The bounty, though; the bounty.

Plenty of the clan did other things, of course. A lot were farming. Uncle Hare sold tractors and farm equipment. Aunt Connie and Aunt Phred ran a daycare; a chain-link fence enclosed the back and side yards of the bungalow Aunt Connie had inherited. I used to spend hours pushing littler kids on the swings or taking them over to the barbed wire fence to greet the horses. The daycare had maybe thirty children, and every morning both women rose at five and got a good head start on lunch before the earliest kids began arriving. Like the food prepared by most everyone I knew, what they cooked was essentially soul food (though our family was pretty much white along every branch we knew about). Our staples were field peas, black-eyed peas, green beans, butterbeans, pork chops, fried chicken. Tomato sandwiches. Biscuits or cornbread, corn on the cob, grits (more corn).

Those sleepy afternoons, and then the genuinely fond goodbyes. "Dale, your mama's here. Give me some sugar before you go. See you tomorrow, baby. Stevie, here's your daddy to get you. Remember your jacket, honey. See you tomorrow."

Those childcare kids were lucky, being nurtured and held and hugged by my loving, no-nonsense aunts, sitting at the long low tables for a lunch of Connie's silky, warm pole beans and a chicken drumstick with one of Phred's buttered biscuits—still the best meal I can imagine, besides Lexington Barbecue, and one I would drive a thousand miles for without stopping if I could somehow be six again and back on that lumpy sofa after a day of first grade in 1970, not yet able to read but contentedly paging through a handed-down Flicka-Ricka-Dicka book while waiting for a parent to come pick me up.

They could manage because there wasn't the regulation. As someone who works in the food industry, I'll agree wholeheartedly that regulation is a good thing. No argument; it saves lives. But. My aunts couldn't have run their daycare without their garden. If Phred and Connie had been prevented from serving the tomatoes they grew, the chicken they bought at just above cost from Uncle Eddie, the molasses my Grandma Vera still made in her shed, they could not have stayed in business.

And while it was once possible to shave expenses because various regulations were not as stringent, so much cost-cutting since then has come via pressure on wages. I was travelling to the Outer Banks with Uncle Keith, maybe ten years ago, and he and I marvelled at the way the South's been paved with fancy shopping plazas. "This entire economy depends on trying to keep the minimum wage unsustainably low, forever," I can remember him pointing out, and I recall the shock that went through me and how fortunate I understood myself to be, working for a family company where they don't think it's wrong if you want to actually live on your salary.

Maybe that's the thing. Maybe humans are too tribal to feel inclined to pay a living wage to someone outside their family. But there's a policy fix for that, and when it comes around, all those retail spaces will empty out again; instead of what they displaced, the fields of lima beans and watermelon and kudzu, or cabins or pine forests, we'll be stuck with darkened empty stores. And what will go in there instead? Urgent care centres and nursing homes?

Kat has often been the cousin I'm closest to, though we hardly saw each other when she was married and living in Oregon. Now she's divorced and back again, and we took up where we'd left off.

Our bond was really formed when we were teenagers; we spent a lot of afternoons at Aunt Pat and Uncle Todd's, which was halfway—a ten-minute walk for each of us. Uncle Todd was a dairy farmer with useful welding skills. He'd rigged up a zipline that went from a high platform and dropped you down into the middle of the pond, and dotted around on the shoreline were his versions of midway rides. I think there were four. A couple had seats that were oil barrels cut down, corroding and blackened; yellow paint flakes the size of my thumb would come loose and fall away as we swung through the air.

I wish I could remember more clearly how his rides were made. The merry-go-round had tractor seats. He used parts and motors, but from what? Balers, combines? Nothing was decorative; it was all battered, greasy, pitted with broken bubbles of rust and welded with long bumpy seams like old toothpaste, and if you forgot to drag on jeans over your wet bathing suit, you'd burn your legs on the sun-heated machinery—or, worse, get cut by a jagged edge. The grownups took such cuts seriously, peering at them closely and saying, "Go wash it good. Use soap, now," and making low-voiced remarks about our tetanus shots being up to date. Our bathing suits would always be ruined, by the end of the summer, with snags and oil stains, but it was worth it.

His contraptions weren't high, but their oddness made them feel dangerous. One ride had not seats but perches, something like a ski hill's T-bar, and we'd travel in a stately loop, all the cousins arching over the bar as far as we could in backbends, then struggling up again to reach the crossbars. We yelled to one another across the screeching, laboring central hub that hauled us in slow circles. All the metal groaned terrifyingly, and the machines were sluggish getting started, then picked up speed. Long arms that Uncle Todd had welded extra well dipped and shuddered, sagging alarmingly toward the ground. No one questioned whether we might be flung to our deaths, whether Todd had the requisite skills for this, whether it was up to code; it was just a more elaborate version of swinging on a gate or jumping from the haymow. People aged out; the jaded older cousins hardly bothered to ride anymore. Kat and I did not suspect that would happen to us.

Going on alone wasn't allowed; an adult or older cousin had to be there to get you settled properly on the ride, start the motor, and make sure it was fully stopped before you climbed down. But there was always someone around who would good-naturedly do it for a while.

When Kat and I stayed over at Aunt Pat and Uncle Todd's house, we slept in our cousin Daniel's old bedroom, with the twin beds a little musty but soft, piled with quilts made by some relative we couldn't remember, and Aunt Pat would make us blackberry French toast for breakfast. Other than that she and Uncle Todd mostly ignored us, letting us have the run of the place as if we were their own kids. We read our way through Daniel's abandoned paperbacks, Dune and Arthur C. Clarke and the dragons of Pern, and we stayed up late in a way that now seems remarkably rude. Once Aunt Pat came out at three in the morning and found us still watching old movies with all the living room lights on. She just told us not to make popcorn this late, but that we could get cereal or ice cream if we were hungry.

Uncle Todd took the equipment down while I was at college or in Europe. It might not have been until his funeral reception that I looked across the backyard and saw the rides had all vanished; slender oak trees, the size of houseplants, were beginning to grow in the spaces the moaning rides had so blackly occupied.

Kat told me one of the problems with her marriage was that she took too long to adjust to it.

"The first couple of years, I still felt entitled to get crushes on other guys," she said. "And it's not like Andrew and I had some open arrangement. I just couldn't wrap my mind around the fact that there was no real transition period. There should be sort of a . . . crumple zone."

"To absorb the shock of the change," I said.

"Exactly," she said. "I loved Andrew and wanted to be with him. I just had that little rebellious streak in the back of my mind, saying, Hey, hang on here. Aren't we going to taper off, first? We were making this new life, new apartment, with the towels and the curtains and the wineglasses, and I still would end up thinking my rights had been curtailed."

"That's weird," I said. I've been married more than twenty years, and I don't remember feeling like that.

"Yeah," she said. "I wouldn't be like that now. I'd know what to expect, beforehand."

"That was your practice round," I said. For a couple of years we spent a fair amount of time poking around on her dating apps when we should have been working. Some terrific prospects turned up, though they were few and far between. Then she met David, who teaches sixth grade and coaches softball and has the summers off; last July they took a cruise to Alaska, and we're all low-key but hopeful.

Kat was so important to me when we were twelve, fourteen, that I admired what she admired, and I automatically wanted what she wanted, sometimes before she even finished her sentences. Once she told me, "I want an army jacket," and I chimed in, "So do I!" as if it were a miraculous coincidence, and in fact it felt like one. Only privately was I guiltily aware that my wish for one had taken hold and fully bloomed while she was saying the words. By the time I assured her we had the same wish, it was a done deal; slouching around the high school, a badass in an army jacket, already seemed like my most long-held ambition. (At that time I believed I wanted to be unique, though clearly this wasn't a top priority.) Copying her felt fraudulent—I understood myself to be deceitful, a cheater—and yet telling her wouldn't have fixed it. There was no sufficiently casual phrasing. I didn't have the language that would have simultaneously been candid about my timing concerning army jackets, and also encompass how very, very badly I now wanted one.

These days I know how to fix this: just say it aloud. Don't overthink. "I never noticed them until the minute you said that, but then it was like I'd always wanted one." Problem solved. Amazing how many years it took me to learn to defuse tricky situations with frankness.

Aunt Theresa and Uncle Ry's younger daughter, Jordan, once told me and Kat that she envied us because we were from the popular side of the family. I was startled by that—was there such a thing? I emulated Kat, but not with a sense that popularity entered into it, or that my aunts and uncles were sorted into any such rankings. In fact, I thought the whole idea of a family, the definition, pretty much repudiated the idea of popular or not-popular. Certainly I had no sense of anyone being in charge, acting as lead decision-maker or chief influencer; we were just a big milling, unorganized clan who still lived near one another, like almost everyone else I went to school with. Your family was your go-to source of employment, socializing, religious insight, houseplant cuttings, cooking and driving instruction, home down-payment loans, romantic advice, and general wisdom and personal feedback on how you were faring with your life goals. Humanity can't have changed, but it's true that families are more scattered now, at least in North America. There must be people for whom the enormous gatherings still happen routinely and without planning, but I don't know where those people live.

And Kat and I, though we made such different choices, have ended up back in the same place, leading basically interchangeable lives. From the outside you'd have trouble telling us apart.

With other regions' news, the difficulty lies in finding a point of access. The surface is slippery and impenetrable, hard to get any purchase on. Sometimes there's one story or individual, one election. One photo, even. But there has to be that starting point and then, equally important, there needs to be some way to fill in the unfamiliar background.

It's easy when it's what you're used to. If, say, Karen Handel runs for office—well, I remember her handing out Zero bars to her staff to underline her plans for Georgia: zero welfare recipients. Or if someone lists Gillibrand, Klobuchar, and Duckworth, I have opinions. When Obamacare changes get bandied about, I still have enough leftover knowledge from the earliest negotiations to kind of grasp the implications. Follow policy developments closely enough at the time (I remember, during those talks, when Tom Daschle got new glasses—I was not getting a whole lot of work done then), and that frontloading can carry you through a lot of news cycles.

There's no way, at least that I've ever found, to tap into that web of information for many other countries.

But they can be bothered to do it with us. So you have Xi Jinping asking, "Who's this Roy Moore?" I understand how they get the information; but where do they find the *time*?

It's now been a decade since the world tipped from mostly rural to predominately urban. My upbringing was unremarkable, and surely I believed somehow that only the remarkable disappears, while the ordinary lasts. That no one cares to steal or alter what's hard to notice. Since we lived in a town, I thought that was my identity: town person. Now I can see how newly scratched in the dirt that life was, how essentially rural it remained. How all of that held me.

On Uncle Todd's peculiar slow rides, so much safer than they looked, we could sense only the six or seven miles an hour we were being moved around at. The underlying speeds were, as always, not just undetectable but beyond comprehension: the racing of the planet, of our arm of the spinning galaxy. Would we be better off if we could feel it?

At dinner my husband, Mark, gave me a new idea about Maura and those weird dreams. He said maybe, since a lot of us in my family favour one another in looks, she's kind of recognizing elderly relatives in my bone structure and so forth. My characteristic familial wrinkles. I'm glad; it's less off-putting to think her dreams aren't crazy. My face is mine, but it's not just mine; other people had it before I did.

I was so heartened, during the years I was chipping away at these stories, to receive support from the Writers' Trust of Canada, the Toronto Arts Council, and the Ontario Arts Council. The OAC grants I received were through *The New Quarterly*, *Descant*, and Cormorant Books, and I'm grateful to the editors there who had kind words for my work.

Notes

"The Voice of Furniture"

- Ottawa's tulip festival takes place each May and is well worth attending.
- The phrase "abandoned all democratic norms and guardrails" comes from David Frum's May 2016 *Atlantic* essay, "The Seven Broken Guardrails of Democracy."

"The Pritzker Prize Livestream"

- The Pritzker Prize for architecture is awarded each spring. (As far as I can tell, it's not always livestreamed.)
- The Pierre Lassonde Pavilion at the Musée national des beaux-arts du Québec (MNBAQ), in Quebec City, is an Office for Metropolitan

Architecture project. OMA partner Shohei Shigematsu led the project, which the firm's website calls "a subtly ambitious, even stealthy, addition to the city." Regular tours offered at the museum include an architectural tour of the pavilion. (The MNBAQ's other buildings include the Charles Baillairgé pavilion, which was once the Quebec City jail and has wonderful brick-walled cells that you can slip into when you need a few minutes of quiet.)

"Volunteer"

- Recent research has shown definitively that house cats and feral cats are killing far more songbirds than anyone realized. Environment Canada scientist Peter Blanchard has put the number of birds killed by cats in Canada alone at somewhere between *100 million and 350 million every year*. More and more people are choosing to keep their pet cats indoors all the time, and some animal shelters now make that a requirement for adopting. (Those who follow Margaret Atwood on social media may know she often mentions the Cats & Birds initiative from Nature Canada, one of the organizations involved with this topic. They offer handy tips and updates.)
- A possible link between toxoplasmosis and risk-taking behaviour was examined in an unforgettable (to nervous types, anyway) *Atlantic* piece by Kathleen McAuliffe, "How Your Cat Is Making You Crazy," in March 2012. The link has been disputed (e.g., in Sara Chodosh's February 2017 *Popular Science* article, "Cat Poop Parasites Don't

Actually Make You Psychotic"). The congenitally anxious weren't reassured.

"Christmas Cranes"

- CBC Radio One's Stephanie Domet launched the storm chips phenomenon when she mentioned on air one day that another blizzard was coming and it was time to stock up. She thereby put a name to a practice that clearly resonated with many people; the phrase became so famous that potato chip company Covered Bridge made it a new variety.

"Binoculars"

- The Oblique Strategies aphorisms by Brian Eno and Peter Schmidt can be purchased as card decks or as apps, and can also be read (for free) online.

"Church Vampires"

- Over a hundred books have been written about the Conservative Resurgence, the Southern Baptist Convention's deliberate, orchestrated rightward shift between 1979 and the mid-1990s. Ruth Graham, of online newsmagazine Slate, is someone regularly writing now about the ways politics and policy are addressed within evangelical denominations.

"Midway"

- Lexington Barbecue isn't in Kentucky; it's in Lexington, North Carolina. I would drive a hundred miles out of the way to eat there.

Martha Wilson's fiction has appeared in *Best Canadian Short Stories 2017*, *Event*, *Grain*, *Canadian Notes & Queries*, and *The New Quarterly*. She has also written for the *New York Times*, *Real Simple*, the *Japan Times*, and the *International Herald-Tribune*.